A REGENCY NOVELLA

DEVOTION
of the HEART

NICHOLE VAN

Fiorenza Publishing

Published by Fiorenza Publishing
Print Edition v1.0

ISBN: 978-1-949863-24-6

To everyone who reads this dedication—
Thank you for your support of my books.
Thank you for being one of the reasons
my fingers keep typing out words.
Just . . . thank you.

"A man does not recover from such
a devotion of the heart to such a woman!
He ought not; he does not."

—Jane Austen, *Persuasion*

1

Mrs. Finchley's nerves committed murder in the end.

The event did not come as a great surprise to Eliza.

Everyone in Rothsbury was well acquainted with the vigorous force of Mrs. Finchley's nerves. And more to the point, Mrs. Finchley herself had long predicted her nerves would be the death of her.

Though Elizabeth Mail *neé* Carter conceded that Mrs. Finchley's nerves led to a figurative death, not a literal one. And it was not so much the lady's nerves themselves, but an unexpected announcement the said nerves precipitated. So perhaps they should be exonerated.

It all began over knitting during the quarterly meeting of the Daughters of Rothsbury Temperance Society. The Society members had gathered in Mrs. Young's front parlor, which had the double advantage of facing south—ensuring plenty of warm autumn sun—and overlooking High Street—ensuring nothing transpired unwitnessed. It was a cheerful, if not overly large, room. Perfect for a group of women to knit caps and sincerely discuss ways to improve the lives of the poor . . .

Eliza nearly smiled at her own wit.

She clearly meant . . . perfect for the ladies to show off their knitting prowess and indulge in a good gossip.

It was, quite frankly, the only reason Eliza delighted in attending. Though not technically a daughter of Rothsbury herself, Eliza had been granted honorary citizen status due to her "upright behavior and ladylike manners."

How those who had known her previously would laugh at such a statement. Eliza Carter a model of decorum? A paragon of lady-ness?

Hah!

But Eliza Carter was long gone, and in her stead was Elizabeth Mail, widow of Sergeant Robert Mail, late of His Majesty's army. Granted, her slide into genteel respectability had been accelerated when Eliza was widowed at the tender age of nineteen, and now, at a much-older twenty-four, she was firmly ensconced among the matrons of the village.

It was a position she carefully worked to maintain. Robert, though a gentleman and her dearest love, had not left her much in the way of worldly possessions. Her reputation and small marriage settlement were the only items between herself and penury. Eliza managed both with careful diligence.

"I have the most delightful news," Mrs. Finchley began, eyes dancing underneath the white lace of her mobcap. She waited expectantly until every head had swung her way, her round body quivering with excitement.

Mrs. Finchley knew how to manage an audience.

Once every eye was fixed upon her, she clasped her hands together and made the announcement: "Our own Lord Swansea is to host a house party at Ambrose Park."

That was, indeed, news.

The entire room stilled. Shocked silence.

Mrs. Finchley beamed, thoroughly satisfied with the reaction.

Lord Swansea was seventy if he was a day, a widower, crotchety, and rarely seen outside the confines of Ambrose Park. When he did leave home, it was to attend Sunday services. And only then when the sun shone and the wind stilled and the vicar was demonstrably dazzled by the honor.

No one visited Lord Swansea. And he visited no one.

More to the point—he *never* hosted parties.

Mrs. Finchley leaned forward. "Naturally, as Lord Swansea's heir, Mr. Edward Forsythe will attend the party."

Well.

Mr. Edward Forsythe had not been seen once during the entire five years of Eliza's residence in Rothsbury, though she had certainly heard plenty about him.

Eliza herself had certainly never set foot inside Ambrose Park. But then, she doubted *any* members of the Daughters of the Rothsbury Temperance Society had seen the interior of Ambrose Park. Lord Swansea was not known for his condescension to those of less exalted rank, particularly genteel widows of little consequence and humble means.

The excited bobbing of Mrs. Finchley's mobcap meant she was not done. "In addition, I have it on good authority that Lord Swansea has invited the grandson of an old friend to visit, as well. This gentleman," the lady continued, her eyes acquiring a conspiratorial gleam, "is a most *illustrious guest*."

More silence.

Mrs. Finchley waited, drawing out the suspense. She would not give up more information without first being prodded. She did have a reputation to maintain.

Eliza felt Mrs. Young sigh beside her.

Mrs. Young was never an eager participant in Mrs. Finchley's games. Exceptionally tall and thin, Mrs. Young was the precise opposite of her short, round friend—a sleek greyhound to Mrs. Finchley's excitable pug. Watching the two friends spar back and forth was the highlight of these meetings.

"Heavens, Mariah," Mrs. Young intoned. "I cannot imagine that Lord Swansea knows anyone of consequence at this point in his life. Besides, Mr. Forsythe has not particularly distinguished himself in recent years, from what I hear. Why should an illustrious guest dance attendance on either gentleman?"

Mrs. Young took in a breath, eyed Mrs. Finchley's rotund quivering, and then said the worst: "Are you *sure* you are not mistaken?"

In lady's speak, the question was the verbal equivalent of a glove slap.

Mrs. Finchley gasped, appropriately wide-eyed and outraged. Eliza echoed her surprise.

Mrs. Young usually had more patience for her friend's idiosyncrasies. But for some reason, today Mrs. Young had jumped all preliminaries and gone straight to challenge.

"I most certainly am sure, Beatrice Young. I have it on the best authority." Mrs. Finchley pressed a shaking hand to her bosom. "You set my poor nerves aquiver with such disdain."

"*Everything* sets your nerves aquiver, Mariah Finchley." Mrs. Young raised her eyebrows, upping the stakes.

Heavens. They had proceeded straight from glove slap to pistols and ten paces at dawn.

"I am not wrong." Two bright spots of color dotted Mrs. Finchley's cheeks. "I heard it just this morning from Lord Swansea's housekeeper."

The entire room exhaled.

Mrs. Finchley rarely named a source. Why give away her methods? And yet, Mrs. Young had drawn it from her.

"Well, out with it then, Mariah." Mrs. Young brandished her figurative pistol.

A pause while Mrs. Finchley fluttered her hands and checked her breathing, ensuring all and sundry noted her distress.

Eliza suppressed a smile. *This* was why she never missed these meetings. Mrs. Young and Mrs. Finchley truly were well matched.

"As I said, the most illustrious guest is the grandson of one of Lord Swansea's oldest friends." Mrs. Finchley pursed her lips, nerves miraculously quelled as she wrested the attention back to herself.

Mrs. Young first rolled her eyes and then rolled her hand. *Get to the point.*

"Lord Swansea's housekeeper says this celebrated guest is a nobleman who has been welcomed at the Prince Regent's dinner table more than once and is famous for his valor at the Battle of Talavera."

Mrs. Finchley waited, allowing her captive audience to absorb the news.

Her pause was not . . . unappreciated.

Eliza's heart beat faster in her chest. *Surely,* Mrs. Finchley could not mean whom Eliza suspected. There were other titled heroes of the Battle of Talavera in Spain, correct?

"Are we to guess at this mystery man's identity, then?" Mrs. Young quipped.

Miss Charity Winters giggled. "If it is the noble hero of Talavera himself, then guessing is not too hard now, is it?"

Eliza closed her eyes, silently begging whatever saint might be listening to spare her this.

Not *him*.

Not now.

But Mrs. Finchley fluttered her nervous hands and said it anyway, "Precisely, Charity. My poor nerves can scarcely stand the excitement. Lord Swansea will soon welcome the handsome, very eligible Duke of Chawton himself."

And *that* was the blow that stopped Eliza's heart, shattering her hopes and dreams into brilliant shards.

A death of sorts.

Eliza's lungs seized. She wrapped an arm around her stomach, attempting to hold herself together.

No. Heavens, no!

All the ladies cooed with delight.

"Does his Grace bring a large party with him?"

Please, no.

"Imagine how beautiful the ladies will be!"

I would rather not.

"Will Lord Swansea hold a ball for the entire town, do you suppose?"

Where has all the air gone?

But . . .

Some sense trickled into Eliza's panicked thoughts. Surely he wasn't coming for her. How would he have discovered her whereabouts? They had covered her tracks most carefully. Rothsbury on the coast of Dorset was a world away from home in the wilds of Yorkshire.

And more to the point . . . why would he care? After all this time? Five years ago, perhaps, he might have run her to ground. But he hadn't then. So why suddenly now?

It must be an unfortunate coincidence.

"Are you quite well, Mrs. Mail? You look as if you have seen a ghost." That last bit was directed at Eliza herself as she sat frozen and unblinking.

For the record, she felt quite ill, indeed. And she would cease being pale as soon as she could convince her heart and lungs to resume their proper functioning.

"She is overcome." Mrs. Finchley nodded, tone grave and somber.

"Ah," several voices said in unison.

"It must be her nerves."

Eliza tightened her hold on her stomach, willing her body to *stopthisrightnow*. She caught a glimpse of herself in the mirror above the fireplace—face white, brown eyes panicked under chestnut hair pulled into a simple bun atop her head.

"You forget," Miss Winters said into the silence. "Sergeant Mail died at Talavera."

A quiet hush fell, as often happened when discussing Robert. The ladies, almost in synchronicity, tilted their heads to the side—a universal sign of "Oh, you poor thing." Miss Winters placed a comforting hand on Eliza's shoulder.

"We know how you mourn Sergeant Mail, even nearly five years on." Mrs. Young patted her knee. "I only wish we all could have known such an amazing man."

Eliza blinked rapidly, her throat too tight.

Oh, Robert.

How had it come to this? When would the pain of his loss ease?

"Yes. The stories you tell of him are inspirational." Mrs. Finchley smiled and then gave a gasp of excitement. "Oh! Perhaps the Duke of Chawton knew him in some way?"

Knew him? *Hah!*

That was funny.

Eliza swallowed back hysterical laughter, still clutching a hand about her waist. Maybe Mrs. Finchley's nerves *were* contagious.

"There, there." Miss Winters rubbed her back. "The loss of one's true love must be ever present."

Truth.

Not a day passed without the melancholy of Robert's absence making itself felt. How she had loved him. How she *still* loved him.

One breath. Two. In. Out.

Eliza clenched her teeth. She simply must endure the duke's coming.

William Thomas Rutherford Trebor.

He was just a man.

Well . . . there *were* a few honorifics behind that name, she supposed.

His Grace the Duke of Chawton.

The Most Honorable the Marquess of Strathclyde.

The Right Honorable the Earl of Flushings.

The Right Honorable Lord Laither.

So . . . perhaps not exactly *just* a man.

She would simply avoid him—which, truthfully, would pose no challenge whatsoever.

Lofty dukes did not typically mingle with genteel widows.

Yes, William Trebor, Duke of Chawton, *et al.* would have no reason to seek out genteel Elizabeth Mail, widow of Robert Mail, sergeant in His Majesty's army, killed in action at Talavera.

Yes. He would come and go, and she would not see nor speak with him.

She had survived the events of five years ago.

She would overcome this, too.

2

How long before he would see her—a day at most? Perhaps two? Well, the length of time did not matter, Liam supposed. He would stay for years, if necessary, to accomplish his goal: find Eliza Carter and settle what needed settling.

This confrontation had been five long years in the making.

William Trebor, Duke of Chawton, tapped a foot, staring unseeing out the soaring diamond-paned Tudor window. His gaze scanned the manicured parterre garden with its geometric, sculpted box hedges, clouds racing overhead.

Three months.

Once he had decided on this course, it had taken him three entire months to track her down. Granted, he hadn't needed to find Eliza himself. He could have hired a Bow Street Runner to locate her. But as a former captain and cavalry officer in His Majesty's army, Liam took pride in doing the deed himself.

Some things could not—*should* not—be delegated.

Locating Eliza was definitely one of them.

He would see her, and she would explain at long last *why* she had done what she did, and he would—

"I trust you find your accommodations amiable enough, Chawton?" Lord Swansea's voice interrupted his thoughts.

Liam turned back to the room. Lined with dark wood paneling and dotted with heavy furniture, the drawing room clearly hadn't changed much in the last two hundred years. Lord Swansea regarded him expectantly from his seat before the cavernous fireplace.

"Of course," Liam replied with a nod of his head. "I thank you for your hospitality."

Lord Swansea grunted, motioning with his cane for a hovering manservant to adjust the blanket on his lap, obviously wanting more warmth despite the roaring fire. His lordship's white hair caught the light, a wispy halo ring encircling the edges of an otherwise bare head.

A small part of Liam felt guilty for imposing on the elderly gentleman. He was frail, hard of hearing, and only mildly interested in the grandson of his old friend, Liam's grandfather, the so-called Lion Duke of Chawton. Though what Lord Swansea lacked in physical strength, he made up in peevish opinion.

The other two men in the room, Edward Forsythe and Nicholas Carter, glanced over at Lord Swansea.

Lord Swansea's nephew and heir, Mr. Edward Forsyth, was all practiced boredom. His attitude contrasted strongly with the riot of expression of his clothing: an orange and pink striped waistcoat under a sky-blue tail coat, not to mention the drama of his high, starched shirt points which rose past his ears and limited his ability to turn his head. Mr. Forsythe had to sit up from his seat and twist his entire body to look at his uncle.

Mr. Nicholas Carter also kept emotion off his face, but then, he was in on Liam's intentions. As Eliza's cousin, Nicholas had been instrumental in helping Liam track her to Rothsbury, pressuring his father—Eliza's uncle and former guardian—into helping them.

Liam and Nicholas had known each other as children but had only recently rekindled their friendship after an encounter at a gentleman's club in London. Nicholas was less wild than the boy Liam remembered, though he *did* still keep the company of men like Edward Forsythe.

"You are too kind, Chawton." Mr. Forsythe twisted back to face Liam, waving a careless hand as he crossed his legs and settled back into the settee. "Ambrose Park can barely be called tolerable. Once it is mine, I shall set about making modernizing improvements—"

"Silence, you young coxcomb." Lord Swansea pounded the floor with his cane. "I am hardly in my dotage, and you will cease this caterwauling about *my* estate. I fully intend to live another thirty years simply to spite you."

Forsythe picked at some imagined fluff on his gold breeches, shrugging off his great-uncle's rebuke. Proving, once again, that those who were most in need of a good scold were least likely to take it to heart.

"The others shall certainly find the house lacking once they arrive," Forsythe muttered.

"I heard that, boy," Lord Swansea harrumphed. "If you find my house lacking, you and your fancy friends can take yourselves off. Chawton"— here he jabbed at Liam with his cane—"you may stay, as your attire indicates you seem to have more sense than this other lot."

Liam exchanged a look with Nicholas. They both stifled a smile. Liam rather liked the old man—more than Mr. Edward Forsythe, in any event.

Liam hardly knew Forsythe. He was an acquaintance of Nicholas. But as Liam's inquiries as to Eliza's whereabouts had led them to Rothsbury, Forsythe had been needed to provide an introduction to the area. It was Nicholas who had encouraged Forsythe to insist on a house party at Ambrose Park.

Currently, Liam had no other information as to Eliza's whereabouts. Just that she was married and living in Rothsbury. He hadn't even learned her husband's name. Granted, Liam could have easily sent his man of affairs to snoop about.

But he was honest enough to admit that he wanted to see her. He wanted to hear her voice as she offered her excuses . . . her explanations.

Of course, he could now throw the weight of his title around and easily dig up answers to his questions himself. But such behavior would give rise to gossip and rife speculation for Eliza. Dukes did not suddenly appear, asking after married, genteel women of moderate means.

Even after everything, Liam had no intention of damaging Eliza's reputation as a married woman, such as it might be. Besides, he knew almost nothing of the man she had married. What would her husband say and do? What repercussions would there be for her? This explained why Nicholas was also keeping his connection with Eliza secret for now. Making that relationship known would surely bring questions that Eliza would prefer *not* to answer. Would Eliza react to seeing her cousin here?

And so, Liam had gone to great lengths to make their meeting appear happenstance. First, contacting Lord Swansea as the grandson of the Lion Duke and hinting that he would be in the area. Then through Nicholas, striking up a casual friendship with Edward Forsythe, who was only too eager to claim the connection, pushing his uncle to formally invite Liam for a visit.

He suppressed a grimace. He should receive a sainthood for this. Eliza merited no such consideration. Not after what she had done.

But Liam was a gentleman, first and last. No matter how deserving, he couldn't bring himself to be purposefully cruel. Not even to Eliza.

Liam clasped his hands behind his back, a small smile touching his lips. "You are too kind, Swansea. Your hospitality is greatly appreciated."

Lord Swansea grunted his approval. "So why are you three here so suddenly? I cannot imagine that my home or company comes highly recommended."

"You do yourself a disservice, my lord." Nicholas smiled, his chestnut hair and dark eyes so like those of Eliza.

"I daresay you are chasing after a woman," Lord Swansea said.

"'Pon rep, Uncle!" Forsythe threw his hands up in disgust and slowly turned himself around to face his uncle, shirt points dangerously close to his eyes. "As if His Grace would have designs of any kind on what passes as a 'lady' in this godforsaken corner of the world."

Liam barely stopped himself from growling at Forsythe's disdain. If he didn't need this popinjay—

"Let the man speak for himself." Lord Swansea tapped his cane on the floor and shifted his gaze to Liam. "Is this about a woman?"

Liam managed to keep his face straight. "A gentleman would never say."

Lord Swansea chuckled. "Ah. Diplomatically stated. It is most definitely about a woman, then. Looking to set up your nursery, eh? It's about time, I say. You sold out of your officer's commission when?"

"Just over six months ago."

Liam's father had passed away last year—making Liam the Duke of Chawton—but it took Liam several months to settle his men, sell his commission, and return home from Spain. From there, he had presented himself before parliament and dealt with pressing estate issues. But the moment he encountered Nicholas with information about Eliza, he was on the scent, tracking her down.

"Well, I wish you luck with your lady, Your Grace." Lord Swansea jabbed with his cane again.

"There is *no* lady, Uncle." Forsythe nearly whined the words.

Forsythe might have been Liam's age, but seven years of war and a world of behavior separated them. Liam felt half a lifetime older.

Besides, there was indeed a lady.

Now, he simply had to flush her out of hiding.

He would not leave Ambrose Park until this business with Eliza was finished, one way or another.

3

There was a girl in his favored spot. Sitting just there, beside a sprawling wild rosebush that covered part of the crumbling abbey ruins.

He tucked his slim volume of Milton under his arm, turning the title inward. Most people didn't understand why he liked books so much—*most people* meaning primarily his father.

But books equaled knowledge. And knowledge equaled new ideas. And new ideas equaled lots of fascinating things to contemplate.

And he very much enjoyed contemplation.

Particularly here in the shade of the ancient abbey, tucked into its cool recesses, resting in the stone seats of the choir where medieval monks would have kept midnight vigil.

But today, instead of the ghosts of monks past, a *girl* perched in the middle of the stone seats.

Well . . . in a way. Strictly speaking, she wasn't sitting *on* the seats.

No.

She had somehow scaled the fragmented stones in her skirts and short boots and now sat on the ruined wall *above* the stone choir, her feet dangling down. Were he to sit in his favorite carved seat, her toes would certainly rest on his cap.

He frowned.

This simply would not do. He came here for contemplation . . . to escape his father's disappointment and read without being chided for his 'unmanly' pursuits. Not to be a footstool for a tomboy clearly younger than his own ten years.

She lifted her head and locked eyes with him as he drew near.

He stopped below her, shading his face as he looked up.

"You are in my spot." His words were just as cross as he felt.

She pursed her lips, clearly unconcerned. She looked down, then right and left. Finally, she shrugged and scooted herself two feet to the left.

"There." She smoothed her skirts. "Now you can sit." She patted the space she had just vacated. Right beside her. Up the wall.

Not in the sensibly placed choir seats below.

His frown deepened, moving into a scowl. "I do not climb walls."

He did not deign to explain himself further. That was one of the first things his father had drilled into him.

Never apologize. Never explain. You are above such things.

Her mouth formed a surprised O.

"Whyever not?" She had a lilting voice. Pert. Chipper. "Climbing is ever so much fun. And besides, the higher you climb, the more you see. Why would you not want to see more?"

He paused, *contemplating* what she had just said.

Her statement had . . . layers.

She angled her head.

"My name is Elizabeth Anne Carter." She studied him, a bird trying to make heads or tails of what it saw. "What is your name?"

He scowled even deeper. That was *not* how introductions were made. Not in the world he inhabited. Moreover . . . he had many names to choose from.

More silence.

They continued to stare at each other.

And then it finally registered. This girl was . . . pretty. Curls the color of roasted chestnuts framed two enormous chocolate eyes, a button nose, and a pointed chin. He supposed she looked like a wood nymph from Greek myth. Logically, that shouldn't have made any difference and yet, for some reason, it changed everything.

It was the nature of being ten years old, he had realized. Things appeared less . . . childlike.

Liam blinked and cleared his throat. "Are you related to Nicholas Carter?" he asked.

Nicholas was a boy who lived nearby. Liam was not allowed to associate with Nicholas Carter, as Mr. Carter was merely a country gentleman without any lofty connections.

And more importantly, Nicholas liked to play cricket and hunt pheasants and had never heard of Milton.

"Yes! Do you know Nicholas? He is my cousin." She smiled, bright and cheery, as if Liam had just given her a grand gift. "Surely you have a name," the girl coaxed. "What does your father call you?"

Aside from 'That Blasted Disappointment'?

"My father calls me Strathclyde," he finally offered.

She instantly puckered her face. "That is a rather different name . . . Strathclyde."

"'Tis a title, not a Christian name . . . my courtesy title, Earl of Strathclyde. Someday, when I become the next duke, my name will change to Chawton."

Her face remained drawn down, absorbing this information.

"I think I understand." She nodded solemnly. "It is like how my mamma called me Eliza, but now that Mamma has gone to sing with the angels, I live with Aunt and Uncle Carter, and they both call me Elizabeth. I have two names, too."

It was not precisely the same. Besides, he had many more than merely two names.

"My given name is William Thomas Rutherford Trebor."

She pursed her mouth. "And does anyone call you William?"

"Just my mother."

A beat.

"When I was very little, my nurse called me Liam," he offered into the silence. "But she returned to Dublin to live with her daughter last year."

He had cried into his pillow every night for a month after Nanna left.

No one had called him Liam since.

"Oh. I see." Her chocolate eyes shone with understanding.

She *did* see.

"No one calls you Liam anymore, just as no one calls me Eliza." She suddenly grinned and shrugged her shoulders. "Well, there's no help for it, I suppose. You must call me Eliza, and I must call you Liam and, that way, we can keep our special names. You for your Nanna and me for my Mamma."

He liked the sound of her voice. He liked that she seemed genuinely interested in him as a person—not a title or a tool or a failure. He liked the sense that no matter what he said about himself, she would smile and easily accept it.

Nanna had been the only other person in his life to do the same.

He missed Nanna.

And because of this, he nodded to his new friend. "I would like that, Eliza."

She beamed at him.

"Now, Liam." She patted the wall beside her one more time. "You really must put down your book and climb up here beside me. You can see to the moors across the valley, and the yellow blooming gorse is ever so beautiful."

And even though he did not particularly enjoy climbing, Liam set his book on the stone seat and scrambled up.

Because, he realized, being 'Liam' with a new friend was perhaps better than solitary contemplation.

4

But, Elizabeth, you promised you would accompany me!" Miss Charity Winters set her teacup down with a decided *clink*, her china-blue eyes wide with distress.

Eliza stifled a sigh, sipping her own tea. Low clouds cast the parlor of her small cottage in a blue gloom, the popping fire in the grate only barely holding back the chill.

Charity was not quite done, however. "My mother's health won't allow her to accompany me, and I cannot attend the assembly ball without a chaperone. You cannot renege now."

Eliza *had* promised Charity weeks ago that she would accompany her. But that was before a certain *person* had decided to visit the region. Eliza had expected her friend to take the news in stride. It was, after all, a simple country assembly ball held in the local guildhall for all and sundry to attend.

What else was Eliza to do? The last three days had been filled with hearing about *him*.

The Duke of Chawton had tipped his hat at elderly Miss Graham in greeting.

The Duke of Chawton had insisted that the vicar and his wife be invited to dinner at Ambrose Park.

The Duke of Chawton had stopped his horse to talk with Mrs. Smith and her son.

Eliza remained indoors, concerned that if she so much as stepped outside, she would encounter him. Avoidance seemed the best policy at this point.

Of course, it was unlikely that Liam would frequent a public assembly ball in unremarkable Rothsbury. Dukes did not condescend to mingle with the myriad of classes who would be in attendance. Heavens, a mere *mister* might have the audacity to speak to His Grace.

An unpretentious man like her Robert—if he had become a duke before meeting his end—would have come. The Liam of old would have come. That Liam—*her* Liam, if she were being honest with herself— would not have hidden behind rigid social protocol.

And given what she was hearing of the Duke of Chawton, she was starting to wonder if her old Liam had shown up here in Rothsbury. Not the cold Stranger Liam of five years ago who had so devastated her.

The way he was popping up all over town made her uneasy about attending the ball.

Of course, Eliza could not say as much to her friend. Charity knew nothing of her life before Rothsbury. No one in their small village did, and Eliza hoped to keep things that way.

"I am genuinely sorry, Charity." Eliza offered her most contrite smile. "But I must see to this matter with my solicitor. I shall only be gone a day or two."

It was a lie, of course. Eliza did not like lying as a general rule, but sometimes a small untruth was necessary.

"Can you not postpone it?" Charity was not going to relent.

"The appointment is already set, you see, and—"

"But the ball promises to be most diverting," Charity interrupted. "My Mr. Thomas will be there. And they say that Lord Swansea may attend and bring the Duke of Chawton with him."

Eliza only barely controlled an involuntary flinch at Liam's name. That was precisely why she could not attend.

"I cannot imagine that Lord Swansea—or His Grace, for that matter—would be interested in a small assembly ball held in Rothsbury, Dorset," Eliza said with a tight smile.

"But I *must* be there."

"Why? Why must you attend?"

"I promised not to tell."

"Charity, I need a better explanation."

Silence.

Charity's face crumpled. "If I do not go, Mr. Thomas will not have a chance to declare himself. He whispered as much to me when we encountered each other at the haberdashers last week. You know we see each other so seldom as is. With his family's obligations, I shall have to wait another three months before setting eyes on him again." Charity dabbed at her eyes. "How shall I bear it? You, of all people, understand what it is to be desperately in love."

Eliza swallowed. She did, indeed.

A day never passed without thoughts of Robert.

Liam's presence in the village had amplified her sorrow, cruelly tearing open her festering wound, rendering the pain of Robert's loss raw and new.

"Please." Charity's eyes swam with sincerity. "Please help me in this."

Eliza forced her thoughts back from the brink of that abyss. This was her life now. Playing respectable widow chaperone to an amiable, but somewhat scattered, young lady.

Oddly enough, she and Charity were nearly of an age but worlds apart in life experiences. Had Eliza ever been so hopeful and naive, so believing in the general goodness of others?

She rather supposed she had. Once upon a time. Before her Liam had turned into Stranger Liam. Before Robert.

Eliza set her teacup down and stood, wandering over to the window. The back window overlooked her small kitchen garden. A large bluff rose beyond, separating the town of Rothsbury from the fury of the ocean beyond.

The lone church of St. Anne stood atop the bluff, abandoned and solitary. The church was much smaller than the abbey ruins where she had met Liam as a child. But St. Anne's Church was a constant reminder of the home she had left behind in Yorkshire.

Eliza had worked so hard to create a life for herself here in Rothsbury. She had her small cottage with a maid for help and companionship. She was respected and respectable. No whiff of scandal or shame had followed her here.

And Eliza desperately needed to keep things that way.

She had spent the past three days terrified of the consequences of Liam appearing on her doorstep. Dukes did not call upon genteel widows unless there was something more afoot. How could she explain a social call from him? What would her neighbors say? Would they still believe her to be virtuous and above reproach if he did call upon her with no seeming prior acquaintance?

Liam could destroy five years' worth of hard work with a few carelessly placed words. She didn't have a way or the means to start over elsewhere. But he had not called upon her, which most likely meant he did not know she was here.

She sternly told herself that she only felt relief at the thought.

Not a smidgen of hurt. Not an ounce of disappointment.

His coming here was simply an unfortunate coincidence.

She had the memories of Robert to cling to—the knowledge that she had once been loved and adored. Not even Stranger Liam could take that from her.

Eliza cast one last look at St. Anne's and turned back to her friend.

"Please, Elizabeth." Charity clutched her hands to her bosom, handkerchief trembling between her white knuckles. "You did promise."

Eliza hated feeling so churlish. Charity had been a true friend to her over the past years and asked for little in return.

Perhaps Eliza could attend the ball if she kept to the shadows and positioned herself with the other matrons in a corner, observing the 'young people' enjoying themselves.

Besides, he would not appear. He had no reason to condescend to such a degree.

5

FOURTEEN YEARS EARLIER

A rap on the window snapped Eliza's head upright.

She looked over to see Liam's face smiling at her. He tapped again, motioning for her to let him in. She flew across the small library and pushed the window open.

"Liam!" she squealed, catching him in a tight hug as he stepped into the room, her exuberance knocking the hat off his head.

He stiffened as he always did when she hugged him, but the hand patting her shoulder and his gruff laugh told her he didn't mind the invasion.

She pulled away and matched his wide grin with one of her own. As usual, he had a book tucked under his arm. His sandy blond hair sported a ringed indentation from his hat and poked out here and there.

"You are all scarecrowy again." She giggled. "Your straw is trying to escape." She darted her hands to his hair, smoothing it down in places and fluffing it out in others.

He had suddenly shot up over the summer—her aunt said that boys did that when they were twelve—so Eliza had to stand on her tiptoes to reach him. At only ten herself, she wondered if she too would grow tall when she reached twelve.

He pushed her hands back and squirmed away, using his book as a shield.

"Enough, Eliza! I already have a mother!" But he laughed as he spoke.

She snorted and snatched his hand. "You must see what I have been doing." She dragged him across the room to the table where she had been sitting.

Eliza loved the cozy library. Lined with bookshelves and illuminated by two enormous floor-to-ceiling windows, the room was bright, cheery, and begged to be sat in for hours on end. Best of all, Nicholas hated reading and so avoided the library at all costs. This turned the library into a sanctuary, free from her cousin's endless teasing.

She wasn't sure what Liam's house was like—as a daughter of a mere country gentleman, she had never been invited inside—but from a distance, it looked to be more castle than house with turrets and ramparts and small windows. She imagined him moving from gloomy room to gloomy room, looking properly sober and ducal while searching for a spot of sun.

But her uncle's house was a model of modern building sensibilities. Though not overly large, it sported classical columns out front and high ceilings inside with symmetrically placed doors and soaring windows. Her house never wanted for daylight. She supposed that was why Liam came so often.

On the days he didn't visit her, she would sneak out to the ancient abbey ruins, hoping to find him there.

"Look what I have been practicing." She swept a hand over the playing cards placed on the table.

He shook his head. "Isn't a library meant for reading?"

"Don't be tiresome."

She placed her hands on her hips and gave him her best set-down look. It was something she had recently learned from observing her aunt, but given how his lips twitched, she supposed the entire effect still needed some work.

Or maybe it was just her. She couldn't bring herself to care if he was tiresome or not. He was just Liam, her best friend, and she liked him no matter his mood.

He looked at the cards for a moment and then cocked his head.

"Who has been teaching you *vingt-et-un*?" he asked, calling the game by its more sophisticated French name rather than the bland English one—twenty-one.

"The vicar and his wife came to dine last evening. Uncle let Nicholas and I watch them play for ha'pennies in the parlor after dinner. I wanted to play it again today just to better understand how the game works, but I fear I keep losing."

His lips twitched again. "You are playing alone. How can you lose?"

Her brow drew down. "Precisely. I find it the oddest puzzle."

That got a laugh out of him, low and breathy. Sometimes she worried that if she weren't around, Liam would never laugh again.

He set his book down and gathered up the playing cards, mischief dancing in his deep blue eyes. Liam never got into mischief—and Eliza always did—so she reveled in this role reversal.

"My tutor taught me to play last year." He nudged his chin, indicating she should take a seat opposite him. "Shall we play?"

She clapped her hands together and sat down, feet tapping. "Shall we play for ha'pennies too?"

He shrugged. "Why not play for truths?"

"What do you mean?"

"Whoever wins the hand gets to ask the other person a question. You must answer truthfully." He waggled a finger at her.

Eliza pondered that for a moment and then nodded her head. "I can't think that I have any secrets. Aunt constantly scolds me that I do not have to say aloud *every* last thought that flits through my head, but sometimes I fear I shall burst if I do not say them. Of course, you are welcome to all my secrets." She narrowed her eyes. "Besides, what makes you think *I* won't win?"

He simply smiled again in reply, gazing at her while he shuffled the cards.

Liam acted as Dealer. He kept one card face down in front of him and turned over a nine of clubs next to it.

Eliza started with the four of spades and a five of hearts. She took a third card—two of diamonds—and then a fourth card—ace of clubs. She pouted and sighed, doing the math in her head. She now had twelve or twenty-two. Of course, that would never do. She asked for a fifth card and ended up with the king of clubs.

Humph. Twenty-two.

Liam turned over his hidden card, revealing the jack of diamonds. Combined with his first card, that made nineteen.

"I win." Liam grinned. "I get a truth."

Eliza sighed and sat on her hands. What would Liam want to know?

"Tell me the naughtiest thing you did this week." He rested his chin on his right palm and stared at her with his too-observant blue eyes.

Eliza felt herself blush. Liam *would* ask that.

"What makes you think I did something naughty this week?"

"Please." He snorted. "I know you, Eliza. Of course you did something."

"Let me think about it." Her strained laugh ended on a resigned sigh.

She looked up at the ceiling, pretending to be thinking. But she already knew the worst thing she had done that week. She just didn't want to see his expression as she told it.

She fixed her gaze on the corner moldings high above. "I spent all of church service on Sunday making faces at your father's back."

Silence.

Liam cleared his throat. "Why did you do that?"

More silence.

She wilted. "Because I overheard him tell you to stop being such a ridiculous ninnyhammer."

Anger shot through her again at the memory. She had been behind Liam and his father walking into the parish church. She had quite clearly heard his father scolding him for shying away from jumping his horse over a fence the day before.

"You are a disgrace to the Trebor family name, boy. I am appalled to have sired such a ridiculous ninnyhammer."

Liam hadn't even so much as flinched at his father's words. His face remained stoic and impassive. Which, somehow, was the worst part of all.

Eliza continued to stare at the ceiling, still refusing to meet Liam's gaze.

"Do—" He cleared his throat again. "D-do you think me a ridiculous ninnyhammer?"

Her head snapped back down. His eyes gazed into hers with his normal intensity.

"Of course not!" she said. "That's why I made faces at your father all through church."

He smiled—a soft, wan thing.

"Well then, I daresay it does not matter what my father thinks."

And somehow, that truth was better than any other she won from him.

6

Eliza slowly fanned herself in the corner.

It was really all too predictable. The very heavens themselves were conspiring against her.

She surveyed the room. The assembly room ball was an absolute crush of bodies. Charity had swayed her in the end to attend. Eliza could not say no when faced with the distress of her friend's tears.

And so, here she was, ensconced in a corner of the old guildhall and trying not to panic. Clearly, the village anticipated seeing a bona fide duke in attendance this evening.

Heaven help her.

Originally a medieval meeting hall for some long disbanded guild, the space had been purchased by the town of Rothsbury generations before and now served as a town hall or theater or courtroom or communal ballroom, depending on the day. With its white plastered walls, dark Tudor cross timbers, and vaulted beamed ceiling, the room was usually too large for most town gatherings.

But not tonight.

Every gentleman farmer and landowner within half a day's journey had come this evening with their wives and, more to the point, eligible daughters in tow. All paying the sixpence entrance fee in hopes of catching a glimpse of a real-life duke.

Oh, that Robert were here. They would have sat in the corner together, laughing over the silliness of all this.

Eliza had taken extra care with her appearance this evening, helping her housemaid iron her best dress—a well-worn green silk several years out of fashion—and spending extra time with her curling tongs.

Vanity? Perhaps.

But if the worst occurred and she had a public altercation with Liam and ended the night in utter disgrace, outcast from all polite society . . .

Mmmm. Perhaps a touch melodramatic, but not far off the mark. Regardless of what happened, Eliza intended to go to her doom well-primped.

It was all any woman could ask.

She and Charity had ridden the short distance into the village proper with the elderly Paulson brothers in their dogcart. Charity had instantly spotted her Mr. Thomas and his cousin and attached herself to them, shooting a grateful look at Eliza.

For her part, Eliza had arrived with a clear plan.

The end of the room opposite the door featured a raised dais platform. Typically, it was lined with chairs, which provided an excellent vantage point for matchmaking mammas to both watch their charges and gather new gossipy tidbits. Eliza intended to choose a chair against the wall, one that afforded a view of both the dance floor with Charity and Mr. Thomas, as well as a clean line of sight to the main entrance, allowing her to take evasive action should Liam deign to appear.

Unfortunately, the crush of bodies instantly turned her careful plan into outright panic.

Charity disappeared into the chock-full room with Mr. Thomas, Eliza's chaperonage forgotten. Eliza considered turning around and walking home, but enough people had seen her arrive, and it was too soon to plead a megrim without raising eyebrows.

She managed to push her way through the crowd to the dais, only to find it equally crammed. Everyone, it seemed, wanted to stand on the raised platform, the better to see the duke *et al.* if he arrived. After much gentle pushing and a few well-placed elbows, Eliza managed to wedge herself into the back corner of the dais.

She was certainly hidden back here, but she also couldn't see a thing past the array of silk dresses, bobbing feathers, and fluttering fans in front of her. Every person was on tiptoe, scanning the room.

Mrs. Young stood tall in the midst of them. The woman surely felt the drawbacks of her height most other days of the year, but in this particular situation, having a seven-inch advantage over the other ladies meant she could clearly see any comings and goings first.

Naturally, Mrs. Finchley demanded minute-by-minute updates, her own head at the level of Mrs. Young's sternum.

"What now, Mrs. Young?" she asked for the twentieth time in the past five minutes.

"Nothing yet, Mrs. Finchley. Just Mrs. Evans arriving with her four daughters. No . . . no, there are *five* daughters this evening. Heavens, she's brought the youngest, too!"

"Pardon? Little Lottie?" Mrs. Finchley looked simultaneously outraged and gleeful at the news.

"Yes."

"She is but fifteen."

"Scandalous, I say." Mrs. Young pursed her lips, still surveying the room. "What are modern morals coming to when a mere child can attend a ball—oh!" She paused, craning to see. "The door has opened again. . . . No one has passed through. . . . It remains open to the night . . ."

Everyone leaned forward, waiting with bated breath.

"Oooohhh!" Mrs. Finchley vigorously fanned herself. "I fear my nerves shall give out before this evening is over."

Eliza almost laughed at the scene. If only Robert were here. They would make merry with all the commotion the Duke of Chawton was causing.

Her old Liam would blush to know the mere thoughts of his coming caused such consternation.

She was quite sure Stranger Liam would not condescend to attend a lowly country assembly ball.

No. Not Stranger Liam.

Duke Liam.

How he would dislike the improper appellation. If he appeared, Duke Liam would offer the room a cold turned shoulder—nothing more.

She ignored the burning in the back of her throat at the thought. She had mourned the loss of her old Liam years ago. No need to revive the pain. It was done. Gone.

She had memories of Robert—memories of being loved, of being enough just as she was. That was all that mattered.

"Well?" Another voice prompted Mrs. Young. "Any news?"

The tall woman's shoulders slumped. "'Tis only the vicar."

"Ah." The gathered crowd all exhaled, deflating as one.

"But . . . wait!" Mrs. Young held out a staying hand. As if any of the gathered ladies were going anywhere. "The door is yet open. The vicar has turned around. He is speaking to someone outside the door. Oh!"

A beat.

"What?" Mrs. Finchley patted Mrs. Young's arm. "What has happened?"

"Oh my!" was Mrs. Young's replied. Her hand fluttered up to her throat.

"Beatrice Young, you must tell us immediately!"

Another pause.

"He has come." Mrs. Young clutched her friend's gloved hand. "Mariah, he has come!"

No!

"He has come! Oh! Oh my!" Mrs. Finchley swayed, her eyes closing.

No! Oh please, no!

"Fetch the smelling salts. I fear she is going down," a voice from the crowd warned.

But Mrs. Finchley's nerves were far too opportunistic to allow her to faint at a moment of such magnitude.

The lady rallied. "Tell us all, Mrs. Young."

Eliza's heart attempted to beat its way out of her chest. This could *not* be happening. It was her worst nightmare made real.

"The Duke of Chawton has arrived with Mr. Forsythe and three other gentlemen." A pause. "And *no* ladies!"

That pronouncement alone sent a hush through the gathered women.

No ladies. No competition. What a boon for them all.

Eliza wrapped an arm around her stomach and fanned her burning face.

"His Grace is now speaking with Sir John as Master of Ceremonies. Of course, he and his party shall be granted admission," Mrs. Young continued. "Heavens! His Grace is every bit as handsome as the vicar said. His coat certainly was tailored by Mr. Weston himself. And I do believe those are gold buttons upon his waistcoat and a diamond pin in his cravat. Such elegance. How kind of him to condescend to join us."

Eliza fanned more vigorously.

All would be well. He would come and be seen by one and all. She would shelter in her corner, all but invisible, until he left. He would never know she had been here. She had to believe that.

But Fate would have none of it.

For just as the thought flitted through her mind, Mrs. Young intoned: "Well! I say! It appears he has requested that the vicar make introductions. He is talking to everyone. And"—Mrs. Young strained to see better—"yes! He is coming this way."

"Oh! Oh!" Mrs. Finchley's eyes rolled to the back of her head.

"Catch her!"

Several hands righted Mrs. Finchley, who made a remarkably rapid recovery. How could she greet a duke if she fainted?

Eliza swallowed the hysterical laughter crawling up her throat.

She truly felt a megrim coming on. Could she plead illness and push her way through the crowd? Could she reach the exit without Liam seeing her? Would he even realize it was her?

Desperate to do something, Eliza stood up and carefully inched her way across the back of the dais, moving toward the opposite side of the room. But the going was too slow, and Eliza did not want to make a scene for fear of rousing *his* attention.

A break in the gathered ladies afforded her a glimpse of the duke's party speaking with Sir John Foxly. Eliza froze, brows instantly drawn down.

Heavens! Was that her cousin Nicholas?

She pursed her lips, leaning around an older couple to see better.

It was Nicholas! The dark head turned her way could only be her cousin. The scoundrel. Had he led Liam to her? Uncle had assured her that Nicholas didn't know her whereabouts. All Nicholas knew was that she had married. That was it.

Liam and Nicholas had never been friends. Why were they traveling together now? Was this just another coincidence or part of a grand preconceived plan?

Blast him.

It had to be coincidence. Nicholas hadn't called upon her, thank goodness. How she would have explained that to her nosy neighbors—

The tall man standing next to Nicholas said something to her cousin, moving into profile—an impossibly familiar profile. Eliza's heart stuttered to a stop.

Oh.

Liam.

Her eyes fluttered closed, pain clogging her throat.

Breathe. Breathe through it.

She opened her eyes, instantly finding him again in the crowd.

She had forgotten how very handsome he was with his straight nose and high cheekbones. Up close, she knew his eyes would be the blue of the ocean on a sunny day. His hair was darker than her memory— more brown now than sandy blond—and his skin tanner than she ever remembered seeing it. His shoulders were broader and carried more muscle.

He was no longer the bookish boy who preferred reading and philosophy over everything else. No. He was a soldier. A man who spent most days on a horse and who had seen and done unspeakable things. A commanding officer. A presence.

For some reason, the sight increased that ache in her throat.

Where had *her* Liam gone? Why had he changed in the end, after promising he never would? She did not recognize him in this aristocratic personage.

Duke Liam, indeed.

He had turned from Sir John and was now bowing to Mr. Walter Pelham, his back partially to her. Blinking rapidly, Eliza turned away before he could see her, pushing through the crowd to the edge of the dais.

In the end, it did not matter *why* he had changed. He had. And she had the memories of Robert's unfailing love to keep her warm.

For now, she simply had to get away.

She had nearly reached the opposite side when a hand snagged her elbow.

"Mrs. Mail! Can you not believe our great fortune?" Mrs. Finchley's excited voice rang in her ear. "You must be in alt to meet His Grace. Do you suppose he knew Sergeant Mail at Talavera?"

Eliza bit her lip. *Ah, Robert. How has it come to this?*

Eliza managed a weak smile. "I am sure His Grace knew a great many men at Talavera. To suppose he might have known my Robert—"

"Nonsense." Mrs. Finchley's hold on her arm tightened, eyes lighting with gleeful intent. "We must ask him."

Twelve Years Earlier

Eliza found him perched atop the ruined choir seats, sitting where they always did.

As ever, his head was bent over a book, allowing her to study him without him seeing. The wind ruffled his sandy-blond hair and caused the enormous rose vine covering the wall beside him to shiver and quake. He was thin and gangly with the awkward elbows and knobby knees of most fourteen-year-old boys.

He looked exactly like her Liam, save for the black band wrapped around his upper arm—a sign of mourning. That was new.

She had not seen him in the two weeks since his mother died. A fortnight ago, Eliza had slipped away and darted across the fields to watch the funeral in the churchyard, hiding herself behind a large hedge.

Liam had stood rigid and unblinking next to his father while the vicar prayed over a dark coffin. He had not cried, though he had bit his lip over and over. But then, she knew he could not cry. His father would whip him for showing such unaristocratic emotion in public.

And so Eliza cried for him, soundlessly wiping her tears from her hiding place in the shrubbery.

Since then, she had come to the abbey ruins every day, knowing eventually he would return here.

She deliberately kicked some stones and snapped twigs as she approached the wall, giving him time to mentally adjust to her presence.

He lifted his head.

The devastation in those haunted blue eyes.

He didn't say anything.

Neither did she.

She climbed the wall and sat beside him, both of them staring over the rolling Yorkshire moors. Slowly, she leaned into him, pulling her legs underneath her skirts and up to her chest, sinking her head onto his shoulder.

Wordlessly, he laced his fingers through hers, clutching her hand tightly in his.

8

Liam was quite sure the entire population of Dorset was crammed into the Rothsbury guildhall.

When the vicar had asked if he would attend the local assembly ball, it had seemed like an excellent place to casually encounter Eliza. He assumed it would be like an officer's ball in Spain. He would show up, meet a few new people, blend into the woodwork, and assess the crowd for Eliza.

He had not anticipated being a prized trophy proudly showcased to the entire village.

He was unused to being seen as a title and rank first and a man second. As a captain in the army, very few had made obsequious gestures toward Captain William Trebor, Lord Strathclyde. Even once his father passed, Liam had moved among his military connections with ease.

But now, every eye was upon him.

Liam resisted the urge to tug on his waistcoat and loosen his strangling cravat. To temper his discomfort, he requested that the vicar introduce him to the local populace. He knew such things were generally *not done.* Surely his father would never have stooped to such common vulgarity as speaking with those of different classes, much less inviting an acquaintance with them.

Liam, however, did not care.

The men he had commanded came from all walks of life. They had been his brothers, and he had lived, fought, and watched them die beside him.

People, in the end, were simply people.

"May I present Mr. and Mrs. Walter Pelham, Your Grace?"

Liam duly bowed the perfect amount—not too much, not too little—precisely as his tutors had drilled him as a child. He exchanged a few words with the couple and then moved on to the next grouping—Mrs. Evans and the five Miss Evanses, each younger than the last.

Heaven help him.

And so it continued around the room. Names and faces ran together. And still he did not see *her.*

Was she not here? Blast it all!

Nicholas slipped away, murmuring that he would keep his eyes out, too. Liam nodded his assent.

He didn't want to damage her reputation by deliberately asking about her. She would be here with her husband. Liam would have to greet the man, smile politely. He forced himself to move past the pain of *that* thought.

He wanted answers. An explanation. Anything to allow him to close that chapter of his life and *finally* move forward.

"Mrs. Finchley, how delightful to see you this evening," the vicar said to a stout matron who had appeared at his side.

Liam swung his head round at the vicar's words, noting Mrs. Finchley. His eyes drifted out to the dancing couples beyond and then abruptly whipped back, his mind screaming at him to notice Mrs. Finchley's companion.

Everything happened slowly. Time moving through sticky honey. All the breath left him in a violent whoosh, like being knocked off horseback and thrown to the ground.

Oh, Eliza.

She met his gaze solemnly, brown eyes shuttered, revealing nothing. So utterly altered, he had not immediately recognized her.

His Eliza.

And yet, so clearly *not* his Eliza.

His Eliza was happiness and cheer. She was sunshine on the dreariest of days. She was laughter and wit and charisma that shone a thousand times brighter than the brightest star.

But this woman? She was a distant memory of that Eliza. She held herself with rigid poise, gloved hands clasped in front of her. Her face was utterly motionless, devoid of expression. She was still lovely—petite and fey—but without an animated personality lighting her aspect, she appeared doll-like—an empty shell to heap meaning upon, not one that had once created his entire universe.

"May I present Mrs. Thomas Finchley and Mrs. Robert Mail, Your Grace?" the good vicar was saying.

Liam bowed out of sheer inborn habit. Eliza had chased every functional thought out of his head, which could be the only explanation for his next words.

"Is Mr. Robert Mail not in attendance this evening?" he asked.

It was the only question that interested him, quite frankly. He wanted to meet the man that Eliza Carter had married.

The silence that met his question was deafening.

Right.

It had been an artless breach of etiquette. He should have inquired about the weather first, he supposed.

Mrs. Finchley fluttered her hands in obvious distress, looking to the vicar for help. For his part, the vicar seemed at a loss for words. He turned to Mrs. Mail—Eliza—who managed a decidedly strained smile. Clearly, something more was amiss.

The vicar cleared his throat. "Sergeant Robert Mail was killed in action at Talavera, Your Grace. In the same battle where you so honorably distinguished yourself."

Mrs. Finchley pressed a trembling hand to her chest. "Mrs. Mail deeply mourned her husband and has been a great credit to our community here in Rothsbury."

"That is most true." The vicar beamed, eager to push past the awkwardness. "We feel it our civic duty to look after all those who have been made widows and fatherless due to this awful strife with Bonaparte."

Their words drifted in and out of Liam's frozen mind. The man had a name.

Sergeant Robert Mail. Killed at Talavera.

Eliza was a widow.

But . . .

Talavera was nearly five years ago. Liam had found out about her marriage just three months before the battle that had turned him into a household name. And to think, her husband had *died* there. She had only been married for a matter of months.

All this time, she had been a widow. Free to write him. To begin a dialogue. To reach out to her childhood friend.

Something.

Anything.

And she had done . . . nothing.

He felt as if he had been shot. That moment when one knew something terrible had just happened, but the pain took a few minutes to catch up.

The agony of *this* wound would be excruciating.

Up to this point, he had convinced himself that perhaps the events of five years ago had not entirely been her choice. She had been young. Perhaps someone had preyed upon her. Perhaps she had been the victim of some double-crossing scoundrel. Perhaps she was trapped in a terrible situation and needed help.

But to know . . . she had been *free* and still had not chosen to talk with him—

Ah.

There it came.

Nauseating pain constricted his lungs and burned his throat.

"Did you not know Sergeant Mail then?" Mrs. Finchley's voice penetrated the fog surrounding his mind.

"Sergeant Mail?" he managed to ask.

"Yes. Sergeant Robert Mail—"

"Heavens, Mrs. Finchley," Eliza laughed, strained. Did she sound panicked? "I cannot imagine that His Grace would have had any dealings with my Robert."

My Robert?

Liam clenched and unclenched his fist, desperate energy pulsing through him, eager for an outlet. She had loved him then . . . Sergeant Robert Mail? Loved him enough to cast off Liam forever?

How could she have been so faithless? How could she have changed so rapidly from the Eliza he knew?

Fortunately, the vicar spoke before Liam said something unforgivable. "Nonsense, Mrs. Mail. You do not give your dear husband enough credit. He may not have been a national hero like His Grace, but Sergeant Mail made a difference in his own way."

"Of course," Mrs. Finchley jumped in. "I still get gooseflesh when I think of the stories you tell of him. How Sergeant Mail beat off a French ambush by triggering a mudslide at great danger to himself."

Liam blinked.

Wait? What had she just said?

"Please, Mrs. Finchley." Eliza darted a glance in his direction. "His Grace cannot be interested in my late husband's exploits."

"You are far too modest, Mrs. Mail." The vicar shook his head. "My only regret is that I was never able to meet Sergeant Mail myself. The tale of the time he strapped a wounded fellow soldier to his back and carried him three miles to a doctor . . ."

"And do not forget the orphans." Mrs. Finchley nodded toward Liam. "Sergeant Mail was sent to escort a group of nuns and orphans to safety by leading them over a mountain pass through enemy territory. 'Twas a remarkable feat of courage and endurance. They said he didn't sleep for five days straight."

The chill started at the base of Liam's neck and shot down his spine with lightning speed. He resisted a shiver.

Those stories sounded familiar. Could they possibly be describing who he thought they were? He contemplated it more. Looking at the entire scene forward and back, assessing from every angle.

Hmmm. Robert Mail, indeed.

Liam snagged Eliza's gaze, forcing her to meet his eyes. She tried to hold her expression firm, but it wavered.

Yes. Something was afoot.

Just when he thought he understood the events of five years ago, the landscape changed. How could she have done this? What was her game?

The orchestra began the first strains of the next set, calling couples to take their places on the floor for a country-dance.

Five years of muddy trails and bloody battles, oceans sailed and miles traveled—all to reach this moment.

Eliza Carter Mail had some explaining to do.

He bowed again. "Mrs. Mail, would you do me the honor of dancing with me?"

NINE YEARS EARLIER

He paced before the ancient wall, back and forth.

The autumn weather had turned chilly, bringing the promise of frost overnight. Clouds raced across the sky, dappling the landscape.

Liam looked down the path. Why did she not come? He was quite desperate to see her.

He knew things had been difficult since her aunt's death at the beginning of summer. Her uncle leaned on her more, and at just fifteen, Eliza had shouldered the burden of caring for the entire Carter household.

A rogue ray of sunlight sneaked past the clouds, illuminating the path through the ruins.

And on cue, Eliza appeared in the column of light. As was typical, her bonnet dangled in one hand, her hair escaping its pins to riot around her face. She had only started wearing her hair up recently, and Liam wasn't quite sure how he felt about it.

He watched her clamber over a low wall, her head down, eyes fixed upon her feet. Finally, she lifted her gaze and noticed him standing there.

It was like the sun breaking through again. Delight and happiness suffused her face. She waved her bonnetted hand exuberantly in greeting.

He waved his hat back. He was smiling just as hugely as she. Studying her figure as she approached, he marveled that another human being could be such a source of happiness for him.

Was that how love worked?

Oh!

He looked at her again. *Really* looked for the first time in . . . ever.

He had thought her sudden maturity related to her aunt's death, and perhaps it was. But at seventeen himself, he realized that she might just be growing up. As was he.

And suddenly everything changed.

As she drew nearer, he saw not his oldest friend, Eliza, but the beautiful, vivacious woman she was becoming. He saw the lovely girl the village boys crowded around after the vicar's Sunday sermon, the youths awkward and stammering instead of teasing.

And . . . Liam *loved* her.

Well, of course he loved her. She was his best friend. No one else was dearer to him, but it was more than just the love of a friend.

He was *in* love with her—as a man loves a woman.

"I am so glad you came," she laughed breathlessly, coming to a stop before him. "I feared I should never escape the cook and our footman. They have been at loggerheads for the last day over who has the task of drying the last of the herbs—"

She stopped mid-sentence and tilted her head to the side, brows drawn down.

"Are you quite all right, Liam?" she asked. "Your expression has gone all crooked."

He had a thousand emotions coursing through him and no idea how to express them. Did she love him, too? As more than a friend?

How could he ask her?

It felt odd to experience a shattering truth and be reluctant to share it with her. They never had any barriers between them.

He held out his arms as an expression of baffled confusion.

She misunderstood.

Eliza dropped her bonnet and closed the two steps between them, wrapping her arms around his waist and burying her face in his cravat.

Well.

He had not been anticipating that. But now that it had happened . . .

He gathered her close, marveling at how small she was. Her personality was always larger than life, and so he simply assumed she was, too.

But here was proof she was not. Petite, she fit perfectly against him, the top of her head barely reaching his chin. He could feel her small hands pressed into the center of his back. Instinctively, he pressed his lips to her hair and then rested his cheek atop her head.

She hugged him on occasion. But never like this. Not a long embrace of comfort and support. Liam could see himself spending hours every day merely holding her.

It flooded him then. Wave after emotional wave.

He loved her.

He adored her.

He never wanted to be parted from her.

"Liam," she said, her voice muffled against his neckcloth. "Are you all right? I think you are shaking." She lifted her head, craning her neck up to meet his gaze.

He didn't release her. And she didn't let him go.

"Twenty-one?" she asked.

It was their code.

Vingt-et-un.

Give me a truth, and I will give you one in return.

Sometimes they played with cards, but nowadays it was simply easier to ask.

He never lied to her. But . . . if she asked for his newly understood revelation . . . he would have to lie.

He did not think she was ready for *this* truth yet.

Perhaps she wouldn't ask it of him.

So he replied, "Twenty-one."

"What has you so upset that you are shaking?" she asked.

Blast.

That had been a little too predictable, he supposed.

Well, you see, Eliza. I suddenly realized that I am madly in love with you and want nothing more than to marry you someday and keep you with me always—

No. That would not do. And so, for the first time, he lied to her.

"My father will not relent," he said. Which was also true and the reason he had wanted to speak with her today.

She deflated. Did she know he was not being truthful? "I am so sorry for it, Liam. I know how badly you want to attend Oxford."

"Yes." He managed a wan smile. "I often think he opposes me simply because he can. What does it matter to him if I attend Oxford? But he wishes to control my every move to prove that he is yet my master."

"What else would he have you do? Nothing?" Anger filled her voice, anger for him and his thwarted dreams.

Liam snorted. "Probably. He said he didn't want a rusticating scholar as a son. He would prefer me to be a high-flying Corinthian, a man's man who cuts a dashing figure through London."

"Like Nicholas?"

Yes. Exactly like Nicholas. "Such a man is the antithesis of myself."

His father had recently censured Liam for speaking with Eliza after encountering her in the village. The duke's gaze had turned thunderous during the carriage ride home, his voice scathing. *"The lower classes are only good for providing us with money or entertainment. She does neither."*

Liam wanted to pummel something every time he relived the memory.

"Four years," she said.

"Four years," he agreed.

That was how long he had left.

Four years until he turned twenty-one and reached the age of majority.

Four years until his father—the powerful Duke of Chawton—could no longer legally control his decisions.

Four years until his sire's opinions no longer mattered.

Granted, his father held his purse strings and could pauper him, but Liam was less concerned about that. As the heir to a dukedom, credit would likely always be within his reach. He would find a way. He was desperate to be his own man.

Everything revolved around twenty-one, it seemed.

"Your turn." She squeezed her arms around his waist. "Ask me for a truth."

Several bounced around his brain. *What do you see yourself doing when you turn twenty-one? Would you be inclined to marry me?*

But she licked her lips after she spoke, and that small action drew all his attention.

He stared at her mouth. Every other thought scattered.

"Have you ever been kissed?" he asked.

She blushed. Vibrant. Scarlet. She did not, however, release him.

She shook her head. "No. You know I haven't, Liam. I would certainly have told you if I had."

Yes. Because they were friends.

"Twenty-one?" she asked again.

He nodded.

She looked at his mouth.

"Do *you* want to kiss me, Liam?"

His throat was utterly dry. He didn't trust himself to speak, and so he nodded again.

She smiled. A smile that was at once triumphant and nervous and excited and so very Eliza.

He swallowed, suddenly terrified.

What if he did this wrong? What if she didn't like it? What if—

"I fear you are thinking too much again, Liam." Her tone gentle.

She slipped a hand from around his waist and cupped his face, her small palm warm on his cheek. Was she trembling? Was he?

He bent down. She popped onto her tiptoes.

Their lips met in the middle.

Soft. Gentle.

Nothing more than the merest brush of sensation.

But he felt that touch everywhere . . . in the pounding of his heart, in the gooseflesh flaring down his spine, in the astonished puff of her breath against his mouth.

Heaven.

It was over far too quickly.

She pulled back, that brilliant smile still in place.

"Twenty-one?" he asked.

She nodded.

"Do you want to kiss again?"

She didn't answer.

She simply reached for him.

10

Eliza was quite sure she was going to wake from this nightmare.
Any moment now, she would blink and sit up in her bed, heart pounding. And she would feel relief that this was simply a dream.

Duke Liam was not here. This could not be happening.

But, no, it was her hand currently tucked into Duke Liam's elbow, and it was her legs that walked beside him onto the dance floor.

She swallowed something painful and acrid in the back of her throat.

Had he come to disgrace her further? Was that his game?

Her Liam would never be this cruel.

But this man, the Duke of Chawton, was unknown to her. No matter that she saw flashes of her Liam in his blue eyes.

He led her to his place in line and then took his place opposite her as Lady Foxly called the dance steps.

The worst of it?

This would be their first dance together. His father had never let his heir mingle with the lower classes in something so gauche as a local assembly room ball. All those years as best friends, and they had never courted, never behaved as a couple might.

Finally, the buzz and hum of the ballroom intruded, pushing through her thoughts.

Every head, every eye . . . was trained on them.

Neighbors whispered with neighbors, heads leaning in, talking behind fans. It appeared Mrs. Finchley had finally succumbed to her nervous excitement, swooning in a faint. Mrs. Young and several other ladies waved smelling salts under Mrs. Finchley's nose while simultaneously darting glances at Eliza and the duke.

Oh, dear.

How was Eliza *ever* going to explain why he had singled her out to her overly curious neighbors?

She wanted to weep her frustration. Or, better yet, pound her fists on one rather ducal chest—

For his part, Liam seemed inured to the hubbub he caused. Probably used to it, curse him. He drilled her with his blue eyes.

It was too much.

Eliza swept her gaze past him, finally noting the man standing to his left.

Nicholas.

Her cousin smiled at her—a typical Nicholas smile that promised mischief and torment and a devil-may-care attitude.

Oh!

It had been annoying at age nine. At age twenty-four, it was downright diabolical.

Her brows came down. She shot him a look that spoke of retribution. Once she got him alone . . . and found a fire poker to beat him with . . . and had arranged an alibi—

Her eyes stung. She wasn't strong enough for this. She could not bravado her way through it.

The music began. Eliza curtsied to Liam. He bowed in return. Elegant. Refined.

They met in the middle, joining hands and walking in a circle, performing their steps.

She could feel his eyes on her. And still she said nothing. How could she speak past the lump in her throat?

Besides, so many little things intruded.

For example, had Liam always been this large? In her memory, he was tall but not so . . . big. She could see the flex and retreat of the muscles in his upper arm as they danced. And he smelled divine. Expensive sandalwood, she supposed. Very ducal. She forced herself not to gulp in greedy breaths of him.

Instead, she focused on his pristine neckcloth with its absurdly large diamond stickpin. Robert would never have worn such a thing, even if he had owned one.

More to the point, *her* Liam would scorn to wear such a thing. But apparently, Duke Liam liked diamonds—

"Smile for heaven's sake, Eliza," he murmured. "I would hate for people to think I am being disagreeable to you."

Without thinking, she lifted her eyes to his.

Gracious.

That was a mistake.

He gazed down at her with a pleasant smile and eyes completely devoid of emotion. Dead eyes. Shuttered and closed. Revealing nothing.

She smiled a wooden, pathetic thing, matching his aloofness.

"Is dancing with me such a chore?" he asked.

Was that amusement in his tone? Bitterness? Or was she simply projecting onto him her own emotions?

No matter. She was not interested in being a mouse to his cat.

"Why are you here, Your Grace? I take it Nicholas led you to me for some reason?"

Was it her imagination, or did his jaw tighten at her polite form of address?

"I might ask the same thing of you, Mrs. Mail?" he replied with equal formality. "Why Rothsbury, I wonder?"

Because it was about as far away from Yorkshire as I could go and still remain on the Isle of Great Britain.

That was her truth, but she did not offer it to him. He was not the man she gave truths to anymore.

She was spared having to answer him as the dance separated them. Eliza turned and found herself facing Nicholas. She kept the same brittle smile on her face.

"Enjoying yourself this evening, Mr. Carter?" she asked. Her words aimed for politeness but landed closer to sarcasm.

Nicholas took her hand, leading her through another series of steps.

"I am, actually," he replied, his expression as pleasant and untroubled as ever.

That was the problem with Nicholas. He was always up for a lark, regardless of the consequences—horse racing, gambling, fisticuffs. Quite simply, Nicholas had a strong aversion to any and all responsibility. He wasn't heartless, per se. He could be genuinely affectionate and warm. He was merely indiscriminate with those emotions and, therefore, carelessly hurt others without thought or remorse.

She expected this behavior from Nicholas but not from Liam. Not *her* Liam, in any case.

Who knew what Duke Liam thought?

"I am glad to see that my suffering this evening is serving some purpose, then." Harsh words spoken through stiff, smiling lips.

"Pardon." Nicholas leaned toward her, all solicitous concern, as if she had asked him about the weather, and he wished to give her a courteous reply.

"Did you and His Grace tire of the pleasures of London and decide to hie yourselves into the country to sport with me?"

To his credit, Nicholas did flinch at that.

Good. Maybe something would get through to him.

The dance separated them, passing her back to Liam. He held her hands, spinning her slowly around, gaze unnervingly focused. She wanted to remain chilly and aloof, unbending to his will.

But she had missed him so much.

And he danced so *well*. Curse him.

"You will not answer my question, then?" he continued, picking up the thread of their conversation. "Why Rothsbury?"

"I shall take it into consideration when you deign to answer mine." Eliza was proud that her voice didn't tremble. "Why are you here?"

Another twirl. And then he passed her off to another gentleman. Two. Three. And back to Liam.

He took her hands in promenade, his shoulder brushing hers. "I should think it obvious why I am here, Eliza." His voice was softer now, words a breath in her ear.

She turned her head, daring to meet his eyes again—blue pools under a midnight sky, gentler than they had been before. Beseeching.

Oh. Perhaps her Liam lurked in there after all—

No.

She didn't want to see her Liam in the Duke of Chawton.

But . . .

It was suddenly so very hard to remember why she should be angry with him. Why she should hate him so.

It had always been like this with Liam. Being near him. Speaking with him. Teasing. Playing.

It was home.

But she had lost her home, figuratively and literally.

And she could not forget—his hand had been the one to shatter it.

LIAM WAS QUITE sure he was living his own personal hell.

He had anticipated Eliza perhaps being upset to see him, defensive of her chosen life or protective of her husband . . . anything but the hurt and angry person hiding behind the frozen smile on her face.

It didn't add up.

They promenaded around the room, every eye fixed upon them. She still refused to answer him.

He bent to her ear, stating again. "You know why I am here, Eliza."

She gritted her teeth. "I sincerely cannot think why."

Now it was his turn to feel disgruntled.

Fine.

If she wanted to play out this little game, he would happily oblige her.

"You married another," he stated. "The name Robert Mail ring any bells with you?"

"Sarcasm does not become you, Your Grace."

"Avoidance does not become *you*, my dear Mrs. Mail."

"I am not your dear *anything*, Your Grace."

She should have run him through with a bayonet. It would have hurt less.

He would know.

His chest heaved, and his eyes focused on a point on the wall opposite. *Exist through the pain.*

A deep breath. Two.

He led her to a stop, holding the promenade position while another group completed the dance forms.

"I simply want to know why," he said at last. "I must be a glutton for punishment, but there you are."

"Why?" Her tone asked for clarification.

"Why marry? And then, once you were widowed, why did you not seek me out?"

And why marry *Robert Mail*, of all people?

He chose not to ask *that* question. Not yet, at any rate. He wasn't quite sure the name meant what he thought it did. It could simply be a coincidence. It wasn't *that* unusual of a name.

"The Eliza I knew would not have behaved as you did five years ago."

She flinched.

Silence.

"That was beneath you, Your Grace," she hissed through smiling, clenched teeth,

Curse her for making him feel the heel. *He* was not the one at fault here.

"Where did *my* Eliza go?" He had to ask it. "The one who was my best friend?"

Her jaw stiffened. She appeared to be blinking back tears.

After everything, the sight should not have tugged at his heart. He thought she had killed that tedious organ years ago. He most certainly did not need it rising from the grave now.

"Why did you betray me, Eliza?" No. That wasn't quite right. "Why did you betray *us?*"

She let out a slow breath of air, her eyes blinking faster now.

The music changed, and he swung her in a circle.

"You were never this cruel." She took the hand he offered, moving through the dance steps, plastering that polite smile on her lips.

"You were never this fickle."

They danced the rest of the set in brittle, smiling silence.

He walked her back to the edge of the floor where the vicar stood. All of Rothsbury, it seemed, waited with bated breath to see what he would do next. Gah, he hated this life. He hated feeling like a circus monkey on display.

She curtsied, polite and proper. He bowed.

"I will call on you tomorrow," he murmured.

Now that they had been introduced and he had danced with her, it shouldn't appear too odd—simply a courtesy call from a man who found a local, respectable widow interesting.

"I cannot think that would be a wise idea—"

"That was not a request. We will finish this conversation once and for all."

11

SEVEN YEARS EARLIER

Eliza stood on the ancient choir wall, desperate for any sight of him. How long would it take? Shouldn't he have come by now?

They both knew it was a desperate bid for hope, a final plea on his father's deaf ears.

They wanted to marry, to begin a life together in truth. But the old duke was adamantly against his heir marrying 'that presumptuous Carter chit.'

Liam had wanted to try one more time.

At long last, she saw him, trudging up the path, his heart clearly leaden in his boots. The slump of his shoulders told her everything she needed to know. The look on his face. Such desolation.

And still his eyes lit to see her. Her dearest, sweetest Liam.

Jumping down from the wall, she ran to him. He opened his arms and swung her in a circle, his mouth finding hers with practiced ease.

He tasted of tears and desperation and . . . goodbye.

He set her down and clasped her face in his hands.

"He has rejected us?" She had to ask it though the answer appeared obvious.

He nodded. "I do not care. We will marry. We simply must wait until I turn twenty-one in two years and reach my majority."

She sniffed. "All will be well, Liam. We can wait. We have time on our side. Uncle is in no hurry to marry me off, and we are both young yet. So we shall wait."

He swallowed.

Oh, dear. There was more, something worse.

She wrapped her arms tightly around his waist, pressing her face into his chest. His arms came around her. She inhaled the smell of him—soap and woodsmoke, leather and wool.

Heavens, how she loved him.

"You can tell me," she whispered. "I can bear it."

"H-he sends me away." His words anguished.

"Pardon?" Eliza pulled back.

"My father has purchased a commission for me. I am to join General Fox's forces in Gibraltar."

All the air whooshed from her in a rasping gust.

"So far away?" she whispered.

"If he could find a way to send me to Australia, he would." He laughed. Short. Bitter. "And as I have not reached my majority, I am still legally his to command. He intends to separate us permanently, I fear."

She hugged him again. "No. I shall not allow it. We are meant for each other, you and I."

He nodded his agreement.

"Come away with me," he murmured against her hair.

"What did you say?" She leaned back against his arms and fixed him with a puzzled look.

"Marry me." Desperation shone from his eyes. "We can leave for Gretna Green tonight. We can legally marry in Scotland without his permission—"

"Liam, my love, we have discussed this over and over. The Church of England does not recognize such marriages—"

"I do not care!"

"But you *will* care when you are a duke and need to have a reputation and wife beyond reproach."

It was an odd role reversal for them. Usually, *he* was the one discouraging her from making a rash decision.

"But—"

"No." She placed a silencing finger on his lips. "We have decided to do this the right way. An officer's commission isn't the worst thing. It will give us an income and a means of support when we *do* marry."

Silence.

She snuggled back into his arms.

"We shall simply wait, as I said." Her voice was muffled against his chest. "We will be affianced and plight our troth."

"Since when have you become so wise?" He sucked in a deep breath and released it slowly. "Two years and I will be free of his control. I will send for you, and we shall never be apart again."

Time and patience. That was all they needed to have.

She relaxed against him, firmly telling her desperate heart that all would be well.

12

Eliza woke in the morning, convinced that he would not come. Surely, the Duke of Chawton had nothing more to say to her.

She steadfastly refused to think of him as her Liam anymore. That man was long dead. Their dance the previous evening had shown her that. She mourned her Liam, just as she mourned her Robert. She probably always would.

But she still dressed with care and breakfasted and then sat in her small parlor, mending a strip of torn lace. Her maid, Sally, was humming in the kitchen, braiding garlic for winter.

A knock sounded at the door.

Eliza set down her mending and stood, a trembling hand at her waist. Sally's footsteps tripped down the central hall.

He had come! Now was the moment of truth.

Mrs. Finchley's loud voice rang down the entrance hallway.

Oh! Or . . . not.

How could Eliza have forgotten? Of course, every person within walking distance would want to hear all the details of her dance with His

Grace. She was the only eligible woman he had danced with all evening. He had led the vicar's wife, as well as Lady Foxly, to the dance floor. Would that he had danced with all five of the Miss Evanses and then swooned into Mrs. Young's arms.

Anything to take the notoriety from herself.

Mrs. Finchley bustled into Eliza's small parlor.

"Mrs. Mail, you have represented us all so well." The lady waggled a gloved finger at Eliza. "His Grace was decidedly smitten, I say."

Mrs. Young swept in behind her friend. "Nonsense, Mariah. You will fill Mrs. Mail's head with expectations. His Grace was merely being polite to one of our own."

"Be that as it may, Beatrice Young, His Grace did not need to condescend to such a degree, and yet he chose to do so with our Mrs. Mail. And then to gaze at her with such intensity while they danced . . ."

Eliza invited the ladies to sit, motioning for Sally to bring them some tea.

Five minutes later, another knock sounded. Her heart sped up. But no, it was just Mrs. Evans and three of her Miss Evanses.

Several hours later, Eliza's door knocker had been thoroughly tested, and each teacup in her house had been used, washed, and reused. She was quite sure every person who lived in a three-mile radius had stopped by to analyze and gossip over the events of the previous evening.

She shut the door behind her last guest and rested her head against the cool wood.

The Duke of Chawton had not called.

She refused to feel disappointed.

Her Liam would have kept his word to come.

Duke Liam? Well, he was a stranger to her. Who knew if he kept his promises?

She needed a walk. Fresh air. Who was she to wait upon a lofty duke who may or may not call? And even if he did call, it would be only to heap ignominy upon her head—something she could very well do without, thank you very much.

She fetched her pelisse and bonnet and grumbled to herself about the perfidy of men—with special consideration given to men of rank—as she laced her half-boots. Which meant she missed the sound of the door knocker.

She descended the narrow staircase while tugging gloves onto her hands, not quite minding the way before her.

She ran into something solid and large with an *oof*.

Two strong hands grasped her uppers arms, steadying her.

Bewildered, Eliza stepped back, only to look up into Liam's shuttered blue eyes. His gaze darted to her pelisse and then back to the bonnet on her head, clearly understanding her intention.

"Trying to escape me, then?" A mocking smile touched his lips. "Was it not enough that you kept your house full of neighbors until a mere hour ago?"

Who was this hard, aloof man? She instantly retreated into formalities.

"Your Grace." She curtsied and fixed her eyes on his glossy Hessian boots.

He sighed.

"Is this your parlor?" He turned and peered through the doorway on the right.

She nodded.

"Let us air what is between us, and I shall never bother you again." He motioned for her to pass into the room before him.

Eliza swallowed back the raw, wet lump in her throat. She finally noticed her maid standing in the background, holding his hat, gloves, and walking stick. The poor girl looked on the verge of fainting.

"Please bring us some tea, Sally," she said.

Eliza walked back into the small parlor, carefully removing the bonnet from her head and pulling the gloves off her hands.

He stood before the fireplace, hands behind his back, slowly pivoting as he studied her space. It was not much of a room—a small settee and two chairs, a sideboard beside a tiny writing table. Humble, surely, when compared to the loftiness of his estates.

She sat at the edge of the settee, folding her hands primly in her lap. She would not break the silence first.

They stared at each other for a long moment.

Part of her hated that he looked like her Liam, that she could still see shades of the nineteen-year-old boy in the haughty aristocrat before her. The same hair that tended to poke out at inopportune moments, the same slightly crooked eyebrows. Unbidden, she noted that his eyes were bloodshot, as if he hadn't slept well.

"We used to talk for hours about nothing at all," he murmured.

"Yes."

"We were the best of friends."

"Yes."

He sighed again.

"Are we to talk in monosyllables, then?" he asked.

Eliza didn't trust herself to speak. She shrugged instead.

"I scarcely know you anymore," he continued. "I was sincere when I asked yesterday evening—where did my Eliza go?"

She looked down at her hands and took in a deep breath. "That girl is long gone. The events of five years ago made sure of that, Your Grace—"

"Liam, Eliza. For heaven's sake, call me Liam."

She made no reply.

More silence.

He looked out the back window with its view to St. Anne's Church.

"You said you would wait." His voice low. "And then you didn't."

Emotion flooded her, scouring in its force.

"How *dare* you accuse me?" She nearly hissed the words. "I had no choice at that point."

"You *had* to marry?"

"Yes! In some form or another."

"And so you chose this Robert Mail fellow?"

"It seemed the only rational decision at the time."

It had. When faced with several choices, each worse than the last, moving to Rothsbury and becoming Robert Mail's wife was the best solution.

A knock at the door interrupted them. Sally entered carrying a tray with a freshly washed teapot, cups, and a plate of biscuits. The tray rattled in her hands as she set it on the sideboard before bobbing a curtsy and backing out the door, eyes darting rapidly between them, obviously memorizing every detail to recount later.

Lovely. Everyone in Rothsbury would know about this visit before it was even concluded.

Neither she nor Liam made a move to pour tea.

Eliza swung her gaze back to him. He looked . . . weary. And sad—so very sad.

And that, more than anything, was most heartrending of all.

LIAM TURNED AWAY from Eliza, studying the uninspired landscape painting above the fireplace mantel.

It hurt too badly to stare into her chocolate-brown eyes.

Even after everything that had transpired, he still loved her. He was honest with himself enough to admit that.

He loved her and probably always would. But after today, he intended to be free of her.

"Tell me about Robert Mail," he finally said, rotating to face her. "The man sounds a tad familiar. He was killed at Talavera?"

She said nothing. She neither denied nor confirmed it. Merely dropped her gaze to her hands.

Ah, Eliza.

That was the final evidence he needed. He wasn't sure if this made everything better or infinitely worse.

"So you decided that I was not good enough for you. You would not wait for *me*. But in practically the next breath, you *married* Robert Mail?"

"Liam—"

"Why prefer Robert Mail over Liam Trebor?" He was tapping his foot now. "Did you simply consider me too *backward* to be your husband?"

Her shoulders stiffened. She clearly understood his meaning.

"Robert Mail was not a stranger to me," she said. "The man Liam Trebor became was."

He ignored the pang her words caused. "And yet I was still known enough to you that you have stolen all my exploits and claimed them for Robert's own. Isn't that what I understood from the vicar and Mrs. Finchley last evening?"

She turned her head away from him.

"Robert Mail was a foolish boy." His words lashed out.

She flinched.

"Shall I tell you all about Robert Mail?" He was pacing now.

She said nothing.

Very well, then. He would play this out.

"Robert Mail was madly in love with his childhood friend—a beautiful, vibrant girl who lit his life with sunshine and happiness. He would have done anything for her. But Robert's father vehemently opposed the match. The girl was too common for his son and heir. And so the old man forced poor Robert to join the military, shipping him off to a small corner of the world, far away from his sweetheart."

Liam paused. Eliza refused to meet his gaze. She wiped a tear from her cheek with shaking fingers.

"Robert had plighted his troth to his love," he continued. "They were prom—" He broke off, his throat closing tight. Deep breath. "They were *promised* to each other. It was a promise he intended to keep."

Liam closed his eyes, fighting for composure. He swallowed once, twice.

"Robert served well in the military, far away from his true love. A year passed and then another. Faithfully, he wrote her. Letters full of news and hope and reassurance. His love wrote him in return. He *lived* for her letters. He thought she did the same."

He stopped, giving himself a moment.

She pulled a handkerchief out of her pocket and dabbed at her cheeks.

"Shall I continue?" he asked.

She nodded, still refusing to meet his eyes.

"Then finally, Robert's twenty-first birthday loomed. At *last*, he would be free from his father's command and could claim his bride. He had watched the time of their separation go from years to months to mere weeks. He wrote to her, ecstatic, bidding her to come join him. And what did he receive in return?"

Liam ran an agitated hand through his hair, pacing now. The memory burned, acrid and bitter.

Eliza's expression remained impassive, her unseeing gaze fixed on his boots.

"He received *silence.* Not a word from his love," he continued. "He wrote letter after letter, each more frantic than the last. Sick with worry, he even contemplated returning home. And then, the worst happened. Just three days after his twenty-first birthday, he received a letter from his beloved's cousin, Nicholas, stating that his love had married another."

Eliza's head snapped upright, eyes instantly drawn down, some unreadable emotion clouding her face. She sprang to life.

"You speak nonsense." She stood, glaring at him. "Are you sure you were not hit over the head at some point, Liam—"

"Hah!" He silenced her with a slice of his hand. "No! I am no longer Liam Trebor to you! I must write my name in reverse and become Robert Mail, it seems. A lovely backwards idea but tossed off when faced with reality. Was the thought of being with me so abhorrent that you had to invent a fictitious husband?"

"Liam, stop! This isn't like you."

"War changes a man, Eliza." He spun away from her, hating the hurt and confusion in her eyes. "Why, Eliza? Why did you do it?"

"I h-had no choice." Her voice an anguished cry.

"No choice? How could you have no *choice* but to betray me?"

She drew one ragged breath behind him. And then another.

"Oh, Liam, I d-didn't betray you."

A long pause. Then . . . a whisper of sound.

"You betrayed *me.*"

13

Five Years Earlier

Eliza wiped a tear from her chin before it could drop onto the paper before her.

How could her eyes still be shedding the blasted things? She ought to have cried herself out days ago. But, no. There were yet more.

She merely had to get through this final letter to Liam. He would understand. He would know what to do.

How had everything gone so wrong?

She rubbed her temples, piecing together the events of the past several days, trying to understand what she could have done differently.

Gah! How could she have been so stupid, so naive? It had all seemed innocuous enough.

Cousin Nicholas had come for a visit with two other friends from London, Mr. Clayton and Mr. Wilmore. She had heard all the rumors about Nicholas and his friends—the gambling, the expensive clothing, the string of accusations from maidservants.

She knew her uncle despaired of his only son. Nicholas had applied to his father several times over the past year to pay his debts, and Uncle had refused, stating that debtor's prison would teach the boy responsibility if nothing else would.

So when Nicholas showed up with his friends, Uncle had firmly declined to house Mr. Clayton and Mr. Wilmore under his roof, claiming Eliza's reputation. The men had grumbled but took themselves off to an inn.

The three men had made merry about the town. Mr. Wilmore, in particular, was known for his wastrel ways. Eliza had carefully steered clear of them, mostly because she found their company obnoxious. But she also knew that if she were to marry Liam, she couldn't have a wisp of scandal attached to her name.

Uncle had escorted her to Lady Cottle's annual garden party. It was usually a light-hearted affair with luncheon on the lawn and boating down the nearby river. Of course, Nicholas and his cronies had finagled an invitation and showed up inebriated.

From there, everything ran into a blur for Eliza.

She had gone down to the river with Miss Jane Smythe to watch the men race boats. But Eliza had lagged behind her friend, reading a recent letter from Liam.

Mr. Wilmore ran past her, snatching the letter from her grasp.

"What drivel have we here?" he taunted, holding the letter high up. "A love letter, perhaps?"

"That is not yours, Mr. Wilmore," she said in her primmest voice.

He scanned its contents, a sly smile on his face. "Why, Miss Carter, it *is* a love letter."

Eliza's cheeks flamed. "Please return my letter, Mr. Wilmore."

He shook his head. "*Tsk, tsk.* Wait until I show the others."

Her affection for Liam was no secret. Everyone knew they were promised, but that didn't mean she wanted his letters to her bandied about town.

With a chuckle, Mr. Wilmore raced toward the river.

Angry, she chased after him, determined to retrieve her letter. Laughing, he darted into one of the boathouses. Without thinking, Eliza followed, stumbling into the dark interior.

"Give me my letter!"

A sound came from outside. Eliza whirled just in time to see the door slam shut. The outside latch tumbled down, followed by the sound of laughter and retreating feet.

Bewildered, she pulled on the door. Locked.

Panic blasted through her. She and Mr. Wilmore were locked in. Together.

She placed both hands on the door, terror-stricken, mentally sorting through her options.

"Here." Mr. Wilmore's voice at her ear. "You can have your letter." He dropped it to the ground before her. She bent and picked it up, turning back to face him.

But his torment was not done. "I suppose I am owed something for returning it, don't you think?"

Before she could reply, he grabbed her about the waist and attempted to kiss her.

Eliza put up a fierce fight. Bless Liam for showing her how to defend herself.

Moments later, she had backed herself against a wall, a small oar in her hand, determined to protect her virtue. For his part, Mr. Wilmore retreated to the opposite side of the boathouse, an amused sneer on his face.

Eliza paused. What to do?

They were locked inside. He had tried to kiss her. What else would he attempt?

Should she yell for help? That could potentially bring hordes of people running to witness her compromising situation.

But would that look worse than someone opening the door and finding her and Mr. Wilmore together as if they had planned a tryst?

Actually, the decision wasn't hard, she supposed.

Accidental entrapment was one thing. Appearing unfaithful to Liam was something else entirely.

She screamed. "Help! Help me!"

Mr. Wilmore flinched. "Hush, you little fool! You will bring everyone running."

That was precisely her aim. She screamed again.

Voices soon arrived. The door opened and Eliza tumbled out, blinking in the bright light, registering that nearly the entire town was there to witness the debacle. She collapsed into her uncle's arms, tears and nerves finally catching up with her.

It was only hours later, once she had returned home and the shock had worn off, that she realized the horror of her situation. She had stumbled out of the boathouse looking ravished and debauched, no matter the reality of the situation.

She was ruined.

Mr. Wilmore's reputation was such that hers could not recover from the association.

Her uncle was incensed with Nicholas and his disregard for her honor.

Eliza did have a small dowry, a legacy from her parents. Not a tremendous sum. It was nothing she countenanced in her potential alliance with Liam, but apparently, it was enough to tempt Mr. Wilmore. Mr. Wilmore applied to her uncle, offering to marry her.

Eliza felt nauseous at the thought.

Marry a man such as that? Never.

Liam would understand. He wouldn't censure her for Mr. Wilmore's rakish behavior. Liam would have a plan for them.

She would write to him, and he would send for her. They would marry, and all this ugliness would be forgotten.

14

I betrayed you?" Liam froze with shock at Eliza's accusation. "You led me to believe you preferred another man. How is that not a betrayal?"

He wanted to hurt something, pound out his rage and frustration. How could she have married another, even a pretend marriage?

Eliza lurched to her feet. "I thought you were different from other men, Liam! I thought you would understand that my actions that day were an accident."

"An accident? How could what transpired be an accident? You acted deliberately!"

"How can you be so cruel?" she raged.

"Me? I thought you had married another. You bade Nicholas return all my letters to you, the ones I had written right around my twenty-first birthday. More specifically, the letters where I asked you to join me and be my wife. He said you never wanted to see me again."

"Nicholas?" Her eyes widened in outrage.

"Yes. Nicholas! I wanted to die at that point. No. It was worse than death. Your death would have been catastrophic, but to think that I had lost your love"—he drew in a shuddering breath—"that was unimaginable agony. I instantly wrote you back, pleading for a better reply, but every letter was returned unopened. I refused to sit in Gibraltar another moment, cosseted by my father's old school chums. I was now of age and could choose my own destiny. I sold my commission and purchased another in a regiment stationed in Spain. I was desperate to get myself killed. The Battle of Talavera was not about my particular bravery. I simply didn't care if I lived or died, and so I took stupid risks in my attempt to save others. It took several years, but I finally decided I wanted to live, if nothing more than to prove your betrayal wrong."

There.

He had said his piece. Let her offer her paltry explanations. Let her laugh and scorn him.

He whirled back to face the fireplace, his throat too clogged with emotion to speak. His harsh breathing resounded through the room.

Eliza gave an unladylike huff behind him. It was a decidedly *Eliza* sound. "I don't understand what *Nicholas* had to do with this. I wrote to you for help," she said. "It was an accident, what happened. I was foolishly trapped in a compromising situation and had been ruined—"

"Pardon?"

"I had been ruined, Liam."

Liam slowly turned around, brows drawn down. Ruined? What was she referring to? She wasn't speaking of her sham marriage but of something else?

"I was desperately alone. I was innocent and needed someone to support me." Her voice so anguished. "But instead of comfort, you sent my letter back with a note. You said you could not abide to think of me so soiled, that a d-duke could not have such a scandal attached to his wife."

All the air suddenly vanished from the room.

No! He had never—

He *would* never—

Eliza's devastated eyes held his.

"You told me to cease all contact with you. Th-that you wanted to forget you had ever known me." Her lips trembled, but her eyes held furious accusation.

Liam's mind raced, trying to make heads or tails of what she said.

"After I received your letter, I didn't believe you. How could you have changed so much? Such cruelty was not the Liam I knew. I wrote you again and again without another word from you. After three months, the letters were returned to me with another note admonishing me in stern language to cease all correspondence. It h-had your *seal*, Liam. How could you be so cruel—" Her voice broke. She swallowed and then continued on a whisper. "I finally believed you. I was so disgraced by that point; I had few options. I did not want a marriage of convenience, but there are ways to have the advantages of marriage without an actual marriage. The number of women widowed in the war is not insignificant. I had money from my parents' estate set aside as a dowry.

"I went to Uncle with a plan. I proposed a sham marriage. If he would allow it, I would take my funds and a married name and start a new life far away from home. Uncle supported me in my decision. He traveled with me here, helping me set up my household and telling all and sundry about my husband, Sergeant Robert Mail. I kept the Liam I had known as my husband." She wiped her cheeks again. "You had died to me, you see. I did not know the person you had become, and so it was easier to pretend that you no longer lived in actuality. Robert Mail *became* Liam Trebor in my mind."

Liam's shoulders deflated. He sank into the settee beside her, hands trembling.

Did he believe her? How could he not? Her words made some sense. But—

"I never wrote such letters to you. I never said those things. I never would have abandoned you." He stared at his hands, unsure what to do. "I heard nothing from you. Nicholas told me you had married someone else. He returned all the letters I had written to you, saying I needed to stop making a fool of myself over another man's wife. I only tracked you down now to free myself from the memory of you. I had to know why you had done what you did. I couldn't move on."

He felt her shift beside him, her body turning to face him. He mirrored her.

"I never received those letters, Liam, the ones you say Nicholas returned. I haven't had any contact with Nicholas in well over five years."

He lifted his head, meeting her eyes.

"I never received your letters, either. Nothing. Not a word." He shook his head. "I would have come running from the farthest corner of the earth to spare you even a moment's pain. You were ruined?" Anger and horror pounded through him. The mere thought of anyone laying a hand on her—

"Yes." She hiccupped and then bit her trembling lip. "It wasn't my fault—"

"Hush. Of course it wasn't. That isn't who you are." He tucked a wayward curl over her ear, his fingers lingering on her jaw and the petal-soft skin there.

The moment stretched and strained. Liam relived the memory of those horrific months in his head. The despair. The disbelief.

Had they been deceived? Betrayed?

Her chocolate eyes softened and pooled. Her shoulders slumped.

Something lifted within her. Or was it him?

It didn't matter because suddenly, there she was, looking right back at him with her heart in her eyes. The girl who waited for him in the shadows of a long-abandoned abbey. The young woman who played *vingt-et-un* and drew him out of his contemplative nature.

The woman he loved.

His Eliza.

"Ah, there is my Liam," she breathed, gaze swimming.

Tentatively, she touched his face, her small fingertips chilled.

"There is my best friend," she continued, eyes roaming over his face. "I thought I had lost you, my love."

My love.

Just hearing those words once more on her tongue.

He snatched her hand, pressing her palm to his lips.

"What happened?" she asked, cupping her opposite hand to his cheek. "How could we have been at such cross-purposes?"

"I do not know."

"You were my soul."

"As you were mine."

She tangled her free hand in his hair.

He leaned into her hand, seeking affection.

Ah. How many lonely nights had he dreamed of this? Her small hands touching him. Her strong spirit supporting him.

"How could you believe I would say such things? That I wouldn't come running if you needed me?" He turned his head and pressed another kiss into her palm. "Of course, I would love you, no matter what happened."

"I didn't believe your letters. Not at first." Her fingers skimmed feather-light over his face. Eyes. Nose. Lips. As if reminding herself that he was real. He was *here.* "But as the months passed and I heard nothing, I started to doubt."

"Never doubt." He leaned forward, kissing her cheek, her temple. "Never doubt my devotion to you."

She clutched his head with both hands and leaned her forehead against his. She hiccupped and laughed and hiccupped again. And then collapsed against his chest, sobbing.

Liam wrapped his arms around her, lifting her to sit on his lap and gathering her close. He understood her tears. They were akin to his own. Tears of joy. Of relief. Of knowing that he had not rejected her. That she had not played him false. He let her emotions rage, cradling her against his chest.

She finally lifted her head. He wiped her wet cheeks dry with his handkerchief.

"Better?" he asked, handing her the handkerchief.

Eliza nodded, blotting her cheeks more thoroughly, still sniffling. She clutched his handkerchief in her hand and snuggled back into his arms, head against his shoulder, legs tucked up against his side.

Years of separation melted away.

Liam crushed her to him. How many times had he held her just like this?

Eliza pressed her face into the curve of his shoulder, breathing in deeply. "How I've missed this."

"I've missed . . . us," he whispered against her hair.

"Us," she repeated.

He tangled the fingers of their free hands together, fitting her palm against his, comparing, assessing. Her hand was so Eliza—petite and fine boned, her delicate creamy skin contrasting with his callouses. But strength flashed in the tendons that flexed as she twined her fingers with his. Endless proof that she was smaller than he and yet a force of nature at the same time.

Would this moment last? Would they be able to recover the relationship they once had? How could he ever bear to be parted from her again—

"Hush." Eliza pulled her hand from his and cupped the side of his head, looking up at him.

Liam frowned down at her. "Pardon?"

"You are thinking too loudly."

Oh.

Emotion clogged his throat. How had he thought it possible to live without her—

"Still thinking." She gave a watery chuckle.

There was only one solution. Liam flexed the arm around her waist, lifting her upward.

Eliza, bless her, had never been slow. She pulled his head down.

Their lips met in the middle.

A heaven of give and take. A language unique to them alone.

A promise of things to come.

Their kiss remained staid for all of thirty seconds.

But then she angled her head and arched upward, her grasp tightening on his hair, pleading—no, *demanding* more.

On a hungry growl, he replied . . . nipping at her top and then her lower lip. She gasped, meeting him kiss for kiss.

He pulled back. Or rather attempted to, but she held him firm, refusing to allow him to retreat. And then kissed the smile on his lips.

"Fair warning." He stroked her cheek. "I refuse to allow anything to come between us again."

"Yes. I could not agree more." She pressed a kiss to his cheek. "But first, I would like to corner Nicholas and demand some explanations."

Liam raised his eyebrows, sitting back slightly.

She patted his shoulder. "You are allowed to hurt him if he is truly the source of our sorrow."

"Me?" Liam flared his eyes in mock astonishment. "You know that isn't my way."

"Fine. I will allow you to hold him down while *I* supply the punishment."

Liam laughed, kissing her soundly. "Ah. Now there is the Eliza I know."

15

Eliza was a woman on a mission.

She donned her bonnet and took Liam's arm as they strolled through town toward Ambrose Park.

Of course, every single person in the village poked a head out a window or door to stare—their own Mrs. Robert Mail walking arm-in-arm with the Duke of Chawton.

But he was *her* Liam, the sweet, kind, loving boy she had known grown to manhood.

Her mind buzzed with questions, trying to sort through the events of five years ago. Liam had never received her letters, had never written her those awful notes. Just as her letters had never reached him.

Nicholas had a hand in it all. It was the only logical explanation. Had he known? And if so, how could he have acted so callously?

She smiled and nodded to her acquaintances. Fortunately, Liam's ducal presence kept most people at bay. She was not in the mood for small talk at present.

Nicholas was not at the inn or the lending library or the haberdasher. He was not at Ambrose Park, but a groom in the stables said he had seen Mr. Carter walking toward St. Anne's Church atop the ocean bluff.

Eliza and Liam strolled along the path to the abandoned church.

"Tell me what transpired five years ago," he said.

And so she did. She recounted the sad tale of Mr. Wilmore and the events surrounding her ruin. Liam clenched his jaw over and over as she spoke, his arm beneath her hand flexing in anger.

"Did Nicholas not call that scoundrel out?" he asked in outrage. "How could your cousin not defend your honor?"

"Things were not so simple, my love. Mr. Wilmore offered for me that very night. He was contrite and apologetic. I refused him. So there was nothing for Nicholas to contest."

Liam scowled. "Your dear cousin should have avoided bringing his friends home in the first place."

Eliza could not fault his logic. "I understand Nicholas has changed for the better in the past few years. He was . . . wild, then—searching for himself, I think. Though it is a pathetic excuse."

"He helped me find you," Liam murmured. "Why betray us and then orchestrate a reunion?"

That was the question.

They walked up the steep path to the church, Liam going before them, her hand clutched tightly in his.

St. Anne's appeared as it always did, enormous at a distance but deceptively small up close. The ruin was charming, however—similar and yet different from the place where they met as children.

Liam helped her through the doorway into the roofless nave. Ivy sprawled across the church walls. Birds quarreled in the walls overhead. Sheep baaed outside.

Nicholas was there, his lean body lounging against the wall at the end of the long central aisle where the altarpiece would have sat, vacant windows soaring above him. He had every appearance of a man who had been waiting for them. A man who knew his guilt and now awaited his fate.

Her cousin watched them approach, his face unreadable. Solemn. Steadfast. He did not greet them. They did not greet him.

Liam pulled to a stop six feet in front of Nicholas, brows a thundercloud.

"Explain to me why I shouldn't call you out and put a bullet through your black heart." Liam's voice carried loudly in the small space.

Nicholas said nothing, face resigned.

A thousand memories assaulted her: Nicholas teasing and tormenting her as a child, Nicholas's mocking comments about Liam and his "bookworm" ways, Nicholas laughing with Mr. Wilmore and his other friends.

"I'm not particularly interested in explanations." Eliza released Liam's arm. "I'm perfectly fine if we go straight to justice."

She took several steps forward.

Crack.

The sound of her palm hitting Nicholas' cheek echoed across the ancient church.

"*That* is for betraying your own flesh and blood," she hissed.

Nicholas didn't react. In fact, he seemed . . . relieved. Which, to Eliza, really seemed like an incorrect emotion for the situation.

But staring into his eyes, she did not see the Nicholas of old. No teasing mischief. No mocking glint.

Instead, she saw a man resolved on his course of action. A man determined to see something through, regardless of the cost.

Eliza's anger deflated.

It was hard to punish a man who would not defend himself and instead viewed the punishment as a type of penitence. *Curse him.*

"I am desperate to make amends for years of folly, Eliza." Nicholas's eyes pleaded with hers. "Allow me to confess my sins, and then you may do with me as you will. Heaven knows I probably deserve it and more." He ran a gloved hand over his face. "I have waited five long years to right this wrong."

"What did you do?" she whispered.

"You must understand, Eliza, I was a different person five years ago." Nicholas angled his head, darting a beseeching glance at Liam behind her. "I behaved foolishly and racked up debts I could not repay. I applied to my father for the funds to cover them, but he refused me. He told me I had gotten myself into the predicament, and I could get myself out of it.

He had no intention of paupering himself over my stupidity. I was angry and, quite frankly, terrified. I knew it was only a matter of time before I ended up in debtor's prison."

"But what does that have to do with us?" Eliza turned halfway, gesturing between herself and Liam.

Liam stared down Nicholas. She knew that look on Liam's face, frustration and heartache. In the past, he only donned that expression when he was dealing with—

Oh!

Eliza's heart sank. She knew the answer even before Nicholas's next words.

"Salvation arrived in the form of a summons." Nicholas fixed his gaze on Liam. "You can imagine who, can you not?"

"My father." Liam's voice was utterly toneless.

"Yes. Your father." Nicholas nodded.

Of course. The previous Duke of Chawton.

Even though she knew the answer, it still felt like a blow to the midriff.

Eliza took a step back and wrapped her arms around Liam's waist. He stood perfectly still. But she knew his heart as well as her own.

This wound hurt.

For his part, Liam returned her embrace, his hand a secure weight on her hip. She closed her eyes, momentarily sinking into his strength. *How* she had missed this. The simple act of someone else supporting her.

Nicholas sighed. "Your father had collected all of my debts, you see. Every last one. He would see me rot in prison, he said, but there was a way free, a way to clear all my debts in one fell swoop. I simply had to ensure his son"—Nicholas motioned toward Liam—"did not marry my cousin, Eliza Carter. I had to convince Eliza to marry another."

"Oh, Nicholas," Eliza breathed, refusing to look at him. "How could you?"

Nicholas laughed, a bitter, harsh sound. "Trust me, Cousin, no one has loathed me more than myself these past years."

Liam ran his free hand over his face. His expression so . . . tired. "Even from the grave, my father tries to destroy every scrap of happiness that comes my way."

"Hush, my love." Eliza squeezed his waist, pressing her face into his chest. "Do not waste another breath on that man. He was an angry person whose only goal was to ensure that others were as miserable as himself. He could not abide happiness because it so highlighted what he lacked."

"You are wise, Cousin Eliza. Wiser than myself." Nicholas stood upright, placing his hands on his hips. "I have wanted to make amends for so long—" His voice broke.

Liam clenched his jaw, gazing at Nicholas and rolling his hand. *Get on with it, then.*

Nicholas deflated. "All those years ago, your father found me eager to do his bidding. I was foolish and desperate. So I concocted a plan, convincing Wilmore that you, Eliza, were a bit of an heiress and easy pickings. I had intended you would marry him—"

Liam growled and took a step toward Nicholas.

Eliza held him back. "Let him finish, my love."

Nicholas didn't react. Just stared at Liam with sad eyes. "Part of me rejoiced when you refused to be cowed into a marriage of convenience, Eliza. But I had to keep you both apart—"

"You took our letters." It was not a question.

Her cousin nodded. "I did. I had an arrangement with Mr. Johnson—"

"The innkeeper?" Liam asked.

"Yes. He acted as postmaster, too. For a small sum, he passed letters on to you, but of course, I was not." Nicholas looked at Liam. "The old duke lent me your seal as Strathclyde, and I was able to create a fair mimicry of your handwriting and pass off notes as your own. Eventually, you both ceased writing each other. Eliza moved away, my father telling us all that she had married someone else. It was only recently that I learned of your true whereabouts, Eliza. I did not know your husband had passed away."

"Why keep silent all these years?" she asked. "You could have written Liam at any time and disclosed the truth."

"The old duke swore me to secrecy. He promised to ruin my entire family if I said or did anything. Besides, you had married and moved away, Eliza. A quick marriage is not uncommon for a woman who has been ruined. I thought the matter done. Marriage is quite final."

Eliza clutched Liam tighter, horrified at how close they had come to never reconciling. All over the foolishness of one boy and the vanity of a bitter man.

"Why now, then?" Liam asked.

"With the old duke's death, I decided to ensure Eliza was well. Then, my father said something in passing that made me think your husband might no longer be among the living, Eliza. It was simple from there to hunt through my father's correspondence and find your exact whereabouts. I could not continue to keep this terrible secret. I *had* to make what amends that I could, particularly if it turned out your husband was, indeed, deceased.

"I went down to London as soon as I heard Chawton had arrived from the continent. I ensured that our paths crossed and mentioned you, Eliza. When Chawton expressed his intent to find you, I called in favors to ensure you were reunited. At least, to allow you to air your grievances and find some peace, if nothing else." He glanced at their arms wrapped around each other and flashed a taut smile. "I can see that you have reconciled."

Liam sucked in a deep breath beside her. Eliza looked up at him askance.

He patted her waist, released her, took four steps forward, and punched Nicholas square in the face. Liam followed up the first blow with two more to the stomach and jaw.

Eliza gasped.

Nicholas sagged against the ancient church wall but, as with Eliza earlier, he made no other move to defend himself.

"I deserved that." He coughed and rubbed his jaw. He would surely sport a purple eye by evening.

"Yes, you did. You deliberately destroyed the happiness of two innocent people to cover your sins." Liam shook his right hand and glared down at her cousin, every inch the commanding army officer dressing down an insubordinate. "You deserve to be flogged within an inch of your life."

Nicholas worked his jaw. "To be honest, I would welcome the pain. My behavior has been inexcusable. I should have come to you at the time with my sorry tale—"

"Yes. You should have." Liam continued to stare Nicholas down. "I am sure we could have found a way to deceive my father, may he rot in his grave."

"I know it is too little, too late, but please know how desperately sorry I am." Nicholas slid down the wall, ending up on his knees atop the mossy flagstones. "I would beg, but I can't bring myself to ask for forgiveness. I am unworthy of it."

"Forgiveness?" Liam snorted, dragging his eyes up and down Nicholas.

Silence hung in the church. Eliza shifted her feet, eyes darting between her cousin on his knees and her love standing tall above him.

Liam opened and closed his fists, chest heaving. He swallowed, his Adam's apple bobbing up and down. Finally, he let out a long, deep breath, raising his head to gaze out the glassless windows of the apse above them.

"My father sent me to war." Liam's voice toneless, quiet. "He forced me into the midst of chaos and horror. I have stood witness to butchery and death on such a scale . . ." He shook his head.

Oh, Liam. My poor love. Eliza's throat tightened.

"Amid all that carnage, I determined that I did not need to *become* the horror myself. Other men felt the same—soldiers on both sides of the conflict. Through their actions, those men showed me that mercy comes in many forms." Liam's shoulders slumped. "I am so *weary* of hate. It eats away at the very fabric of life. My father . . . *that man* . . . does not have my forgiveness for his part in this. But you—"

Liam pointed a finger at Nicholas.

Her cousin flinched.

"You . . . I can eventually forgive." Liam held out his hand, a gesture of pardon.

Nicholas looked at Liam's outstretched palm. "I do not deserve your mercy."

"I know." Liam nodded. "But then, none of us deserve mercy when it is granted."

Nicholas took the offered hand, and Liam pulled him to his feet.

"Thank you." Nicholas bowed over Liam's hand, voice hoarse. "I-I have carried this burden for so long, a simple thank-you hardly seems enough."

"It is enough. I do not want to waste another moment feeling bitter over what has passed. I simply want to be grateful for the future I see ahead."

"Thank you, Your Grace. I don't know how to repay you."

Liam jerked his chin. "You can start by taking yourself off. I have things I want to say to Eliza."

Nicholas offered her a quick bow and took his leave.

Eliza turned to Liam, eyebrows raised.

He stared at her, her Liam of old. He doffed his hat, tossing it atop a pile of stones. He walked toward her, eyes smiling.

Eliza laughed, years of separation and heartache melting away. How she adored this man.

He stopped in front of her.

"Twenty-one?" he asked.

She smiled and nodded.

"Do you love me?"

Her smile went from wide to giddy.

"Yes, Liam Trebor, I do love you." She paused. "Do you love me?"

Now it was his turn to smile.

"What do you think?" He closed the distance between them, swinging her into his arms.

Eliza clasped her hands around his neck, pressing her nose into the space between his ear and jaw, chuckling into his throat.

Liam set her down, resting his forehead against hers. "You once married the pretend Robert Mail. Do you think you could marry the real Liam Trebor?"

Eliza tried to laugh, but it came out a choked sob.

"Yes." Words whispered against his mouth. "Absolutely yes!"

"I love you, Eliza. I never stopped loving you. Even at my most bitter, when I thought I hated you, I loved you."

Eliza didn't reply.

She simply popped up on her tiptoes and kissed him.

Kissed the shy, quiet boy he had been.

Kissed the man she had thought lost to her.

Kissed her best friend come home.

EPILOGUE

W ell, Mrs. Young? What do you see?" Mrs. Finchley tapped her tall friend on the shoulder.

For her part, Mrs. Young stood on tiptoe, trying valiantly to see inside the church without being too obvious about it.

Word had spread quickly through Rothsbury. The Duke of Chawton had left overnight and returned two days later with a special license.

Mrs. Robert Mail had been seen more than once out walking in the company of His Grace, and the duke had called on her multiple times. Was one of their own to become a duchess? How the mind boggled at the thought.

"Well?" Mrs. Finchley hissed.

"Oh! Oh my!" Mrs. Young murmured, eyes peering inside.

"So help me, Beatrice Young, you tell me right now—"

"The vicar is marrying them. Only the vicar, his wife, and Mr. Nicholas Carter are in attendance. And His Grace and Mrs. Mail, of course."

"The vicar is marrying them?"

"Yes, t'would appear so. They are exchanging rings." Silence for a moment. "Mrs. Mail is wiping away tears. Oh! And so is His Grace." Mrs. Young's voice went all wobbly.

"You cannot cry now, Beatrice," Mrs. Finchley admonished. "You must keep your eyes clear."

"It's simply too beautiful, Mariah," Mrs. Young whispered. "I had always hoped that Mrs. Mail would find it in her heart to love again. Sergeant Mail meant so much to her. And here she is, receiving a second chance at love."

"I knew something important would happen with His Grace coming to town. My nerves told me so."

Mrs. Young turned away from the window, studying her oldest friend. "Well, for once, your nerves have done a good deed. Now come. The newlywed couple will be exiting the church any moment, and I have prepared a small bag of rice for us to throw."

"Do you suppose His Grace and the new duchess will live happily ever after?"

Mrs. Young laughed. "Given how he looked at her just now? I think their mutual happiness is guaranteed."

OTHER BOOKS BY NICHOLE VAN

THE EARLS OF CAIRNFELL

A Tartan Love (July 2025)
A Lass Beloved (Winter 2026)
A Highland Game (Summer 2026)
A Laird Undone (Winter 2027)

THE PENN-LEITHS OF THISTLE MUIR

Love Practically
Adjacent But Only Just
One Kiss Alone
A Heart Sufficient
A Heart Devoted

THE BROTHERHOOD OF THE BLACK TARTAN

Suffering the Scot
Romancing the Rake
Loving a Lady
Making the Marquess
Remembering Jamie

OTHER REGENCY ROMANCES

Seeing Miss Heartstone
Devotion of the Heart
Remains of Love (a novella included in *Summer in the Highlands*)

BROTHERS *MALEDETTI*

Lovers and Madmen
Gladly Beyond
Love's Shadow
Lightning Struck
A Madness Most Discreet

THE HOUSE OF OAK

Intertwine
Divine
Clandestine
Refine
Outshine

Want more historical romance from Nichole Van?
Read on for an excerpt from *Love Practically*,
book one in The Penn-Leith's of Thistle Muir series.

LOVE PRACTICALLY

It is a truth universally acknowledged that a single lady in possession of no fortune must long to marry a duke's son.

Unfortunately, Miss Leah Penn-Leith feared she had inadvertently killed one instead.

She stared down at the unmoving form of Lieutenant Lord Dennis Battleton illuminated in the firelight. He lay slumped beside her bedroom door, eyes closed, head tilted toward the left shoulder of his red regimental coat, blood trickling from his nose.

What have I done? WhathaveIdone?!

Panic tasted acrid, drying her throat.

This might be her first time attending a house party, but even Leah knew an evening of whist and laughter did not typically end in homicide.

Clutching her night rail to her chest, Leah nudged Lord Dennis's Hessian boot, jiggling the tassel.

"My lord?" she whispered.

Nothing.

Snick.

The door to her bedchamber opened.

Leah stifled a startled scream and jumped back, meeting the gaze of Mr. Fox Carnegie, Lord Dennis's close friend.

Mr. Carnegie peered into the room, skimming over her surely terrified expression, before spotting Lord Dennis's supine form beside the door jamb.

"Blast," he muttered and mumbled a string of profanity that Leah supposed would make a gently-bred lady swoon.

As she was not *quite* a gently-bred lady, she withstood the swearing with equanimity.

After all, the situation quite merited it.

Mr. Carnegie stepped into her bedchamber, quietly closing the door behind himself. It was scandalous for him to be in her room, but then so was killing a duke's son, so Leah figured the horse had already bolted from the barn.

"I-I didnae mean tae hurt him," Leah stammered on a whisper, her Scottish brogue deepening in her distress. "I awoke as he was trying tae climb into my bed. I just . . . reacted." She mimed a kicking motion.

It had been a terrifying few seconds.

First, waking to feel large hands on her hips, the smell of brandy, and murmured slurred words, "I sh-shink you've been waiting for me, love."

Then, her instinctively violent reaction, balling her body and kicking the unknown man with both feet, much like a bucking horse. Her aim had been true.

The man had staggered back, his head and shoulders hitting the wall with a resounding *thud* that rattled her bedchamber door.

Leah had scrambled out of bed, finally getting a good look at her assailant, horrified to realize she had attacked a duke's son—Lord Dennis Battleton.

Now she watched as Mr. Carnegie stooped and placed an ear to Lord Dennis's chest.

"His heart is strong," he said, voice low.

Leah nearly sobbed in relief.

Mr. Carnegie pulled back one of his friend's eyelids, studying the pupils for a second, and inspected Lord Dennis's head for more injuries.

"Why is he yet unconscious?" Leah whispered.

"I fear Lord Dennis was exceptionally deep in his cups tonight." Mr. Carnegie pulled out a handkerchief and wiped the blood dripping from his friend's nose. "The bump to the head simply sent him to sleep a mite sooner than the brandy."

For his part, Mr. Carnegie did not appear inebriated, though the smell of alcohol lingered on him as well.

"I simply need to remove Dennis from your bedchamber with no one the wiser and leave you with my most abject apologies for this unwelcome intrusion." He flashed her a grim smile, the world-weary expression at odds with his youthful face. "We must ensure this mishap does not damage your reputation nor set gossiping tongues to wagg—"

A scuffle of footsteps in the hall outside had Mr. Carnegie turning his head and muttering another low oath.

Moving quickly, he straddled his friend, wrapped his arms around the man's chest, and heaved him upright. Not unlike Leah's father hefting a fat ewe for sheering.

In short, it was an impressive feat of physical strength.

Mr. Carnegie pivoted, spinning himself and Lord Dennis around, stopping just behind Leah's bedchamber door as a knock sounded.

Leah didn't know whether to be impressed by Mr. Carnegie's quick reaction or appalled at the smooth, practiced nature of it. This was clearly not the first time Mr. Carnegie had lifted the leaden weight of a drunken friend.

Mr. Carnegie jerked his head toward the door, indicating she should answer it.

Nodding, Leah snatched a shawl from the foot of her bed, wrapping it around her shoulders. She cracked open the door.

Miss Smith and Miss Wells—two fellow guests—stood in the hallway wearing elegant London wrappers, night caps, and matching expressions of faux worry.

"Are you quite all right, Miss Penn-Leith?" Miss Smith asked, her blond braid gleaming even in the dim light.

"Yes," Miss Wells added. "We heard a *terrible* thump."

The ladies peered beyond Leah's shoulders, searching the room as if they somehow knew there were two young gentlemen concealed behind Leah's bedchamber door.

"I apologize if I gave anyone a fright." Leah pulled the shawl tighter around her shoulders and mentally grasped for a plausible lie. "I was up reading late—Miss Austen's works are so captivating, ye ken—and I stumbled over my own *muckle* foot as I was getting into bed."

As a falsehood, it wasn't particularly good.

"*Muckle?*" Miss Smith wrinkled her dainty nose. "You Scots use the oddest words."

Miss Wells giggled, standing on tiptoe, unabashedly craning her neck to see more of the bedchamber.

In Leah's peripheral vision, Mr. Carnegie made a rolling motion with one hand. *Get on with it.*

"I thank ye both for your concern," Leah began closing the door, "but all is well. I shall bid ye goodnight."

The ladies murmured a reply, and Leah shut the door fully, throwing the lock.

Now what?

Turning back to Mr. Carnegie, she watched as he eased Lord Dennis back to the floor.

"Clever," he whispered, chin gesturing toward the door. "You are a quick study."

Leah blushed. The unexpected praise sent a jolt of pleasure through her still-racing heart. Until this moment, she had never considered that her good sense and quick thinking could be used to conceal an illicit assignation and attempted homicide.

She wasn't sure whether to be proud or appalled.

Oblivious to the uproar he had caused, Lord Dennis emitted a blissful, sleepy snore.

Because . . . of course, he did.

Mr. Carnegie stepped past Leah, placing an ear to her bedroom door.

"They're still nattering on," he murmured. "We'll have to wait."

Miss Smith and Miss Well's breathy giggles sounded outside as if to emphasize the point.

With a sigh, Mr. Carnegie sank down beside Lord Dennis, shoulders against the wall, wrists resting on the raised knees of his white breeches. Lord Dennis—dark-haired, stubble-cheeked, flush-nosed—snored again, snuffling in his sleep.

Leah stared down at them, unsure of the social mores when entertaining two gentlemen in her bedchamber.

Two gentlemen.

In. Her. Bedchamber.

Her mind stuttered. Surely this exemplified the sort of lascivious behavior Aunt Leith had warned her abounded in London.

Leah busied herself, stirring the fire to life and lighting a lamp on the wee writing desk. She rotated the desk chair—a worn wooden Windsor— to face Mr. Carnegie and sat gingerly, pulling her shawl tight around her shoulders and tucking her toes under the hem of her night rail.

Mr. Carnegie watched her, the lamplight flickering in his pale gaze and turning his blond hair into molten gold. His eyes were intensely blue, she noted. The color of Loch Muick on a cloudless day.

Unlike Lord Dennis, Mr. Carnegie no longer wore his coat. Instead, he sat against the wall in the red waistcoat of a regimental officer, his white shirt sleeves cuffed to the elbow. Swallowing, he tugged at his dark neckcloth, loosening and mussing it. Leah tried (and failed) not to stare at the shadowy outline of lean muscle rippling under the fine linen of his shirt as he moved.

No wonder gentlemen were required to remain precisely dressed at all times. A disheveled man invited all sorts of salacious thoughts. At the moment, Leah was hard-pressed to concentrate on anything other than the marvelous flex and pull of tendons across his bare forearms.

But then, Mr. Fox Carnegie had been drawing her eyes all week.

Leah was attending the house party—hosted by an English cousin, Mrs. Gordon—as Aunt Leith's companion. It was all part of the campaign to lift Leah out of the 'unfortunate circumstances of Isobel's marriage.' That, of course, referred to Leah's deceased mother, Isobel Leith, who had married John Penn, a Scottish gentleman farmer well below her aristocratic station.

This meant that while more refined young women were stitching samplers and perfecting their posture in a side-saddle, Leah had been darning her younger brothers' socks and galloping across the Angus glens astride her favorite gelding, helping her father and his shepherds track lost sheep.

Unfortunately, sock-darning and sheep-wrangling were not activities that gentlemen appreciated in a well-bred young lady.

But that did not deter Aunt Leith. She ruthlessly polished Leah's manners, intending to find her niece a more appropriate husband than 'some half-drunk Scottish blacksmith.' Though if Aunt Leith had actually *met* the blacksmith in Fettermill with his bulky muscles and charming wink, she would not so cavalierly dismiss the idea.

Regardless, at scarcely eighteen years old herself, Leah was at a loss as to what men *did* want in a bride. Well, aside from a large dowry and, perhaps, an equally out-sized bosom—facts she had gleaned from Miss Wells and Miss Smith as they sat giggling over luncheon.

Leah possessed none of those things—a dowry, large bosoms, or a preponderance of giggles.

But this obvious lack had not stopped her from noticing Mr. Fox Carnegie.

He had arrived in a burst of ribald laughter and youthful scuffling—Lord Dennis's, not his own. Mr. Carnegie had stood behind his friend, arms folded, expression wry and watchful. There had been a quiet sense of *noticing* about him, a steadiness that had instantly drawn Leah in.

Granted, it hadn't hurt that he looked remarkably dashing in the red coat of the 64th Regiment of Foot. The crimson wool caught the auburn highlights in his blond hair and accentuated the sharp line of his jaw. Her eyes had stubbornly followed him—noting the liquid grace of his walk, the way his shoulders tilted toward a person as he listened, the kind gentleness in his tone.

Not that Mr. Carnegie had spared a glance for the awkwardly shy Scottish lass Leah knew herself to be. None of the gentlemen in attendance did.

Though . . . Mr. Carnegie appeared to be noticing her now.

In the lamplight, his gaze skimmed her, likely taking in the unadorned linen of her night rail, the homespun wool of her thick stockings, the tattered edge of her shawl. She pulled the garment closer.

Leah knew her features were a study in nondeterminate mediocrity—bland and vacillating. Her hair was not quite blond, nor brown, nor auburn, but some unflattering mix of the three. Her hazel eyes changed color with her moods—brown to green and back again. The rest of her—body, bosom, height—remained stubbornly average.

If Mr. Carnegie found her lacking, his expression didn't show it.

He cleared his throat. "You seem to have the advantage of me, Miss . . ." His voice drifted off, a ruddy flush climbing his cheeks. "I know we were likely introduced, but my memory for faces is not the best, and I fear with all that has happened, your name has plum slipped my mind."

He said the words kindly, but Leah experienced a sinking sensation nonetheless.

She was forgettable. She knew this, and yet . . .

"Miss Leah Penn-Leith, at your service, Mr. Carnegie."

He winced. "Of course, you have the manners to remember my name."

"As your Christian name is Fox, it does have a tendency tae stick."

He smiled at that, teeth flashing and sending a zing of pleasure chasing her spine. The sensation was akin to winning first place in the jam-making contest at the Fettermill Summer Fair. (Which she had done. Twice.)

More to the point, his grin rendered him boyish and young, too young to be in a soldier's uniform. Was Mr. Carnegie even older than herself?

"I must apologize for Lord Dennis." He nodded toward his friend, sleeping beside him. "I fear he mistook your room for . . . another's."

"Another lady?" The thought was rather shocking. That Lord Dennis would have entered a woman's room, crawled into bed with her, and the lady would have . . . welcomed it?

Lascivious, indeed.

"I shall say nothing more upon the matter, as it involves some delicacy, as you might imagine."

Well, Leah *hadn't* been imagining it, but now . . .

Her eyes dropped to the long fingers dangling over his knees. What if it had been Mr. Carnegie's gentle hands reaching for her? Would she have pulled away so quickly?

She looked away, a blush scalding her skin.

"Regardless," he continued quietly, thankfully oblivious to her wayward thoughts, "I noticed when we parted that Lord Dennis had gone down the wrong corridor, so I followed hi—"

Wham!

Another door banged down the hallway, causing them both to jump.

Someone giggled.

Mr. Carnegie frowned and sent a speaking glance toward the door. "I fear it might be a while before we can make an escape unseen, Miss Penn-Leith." He nudged Lord Dennis's prone body with his foot.

Leah nodded.

They sat in silence for a moment. It was a companionable sort of thing, as if they were comrades in arms, waiting to complete an important tactical mission.

Having been raised by a stoically silent father, Leah understood that silence was often a conversation unto itself.

Sometimes it could be as soothing as an embrace, as understanding as a long *blether*.

Other times, silence was a noisy thing—loud and shouty and demanding attention.

Not everyone was fluent in the language of silence, but Mr. Carnegie appeared to have mastered it. Quiet felt peaceful in his presence.

Leah liked him all the more for it.

The scent of shaving soap and sandalwood drifted over her. It was a remarkably masculine smell, the sort that rendered a young woman weak-kneed and pliable, willing to make all sorts of poor decisions.

Keep your wits about ye, Leah!

"So . . ." she began, floundering for a topic, "uhmmm, *Fox* . . . that is an unusual given name."

"I suppose," he snorted. "My father was quite fond of Mr. Charles Fox's politics. I was named in his honor."

Leah was unsure how to respond. The name *Charles Fox* was vaguely familiar. Hadn't Mr. Jamieson, the town glazier, once said something rather crude about Mr. Fox when he thought no women were present?

"He was always a bit of a radical, Mr. Fox," Mr. Carnegie continued as if he, too, were eager to have a topic to discuss. "He championed revolution, hated imperialistic warmongering, and detested our current Hanoverian kings. My father was rather passionate about Mr. Fox's pacifistic views and democratic principles."

Something caught in Leah's chest at that.

My father was. Past tense.

She understood something about a past-tense parent.

"Do ye share your father's views then?" she asked, looking pointedly at the brass buttons on his regimental waistcoat, at the monarchy and imperialism they represented.

He followed her gaze, plucking at the sturdy red wool.

"It hardly matters now, I suppose." He shrugged and looked away, the lamplight casting his profile in stark shadow upon the wall behind.

Footsteps echoed down the hallway, drifting away from her door. Lord Dennis muttered in his sleep.

"How did ye end up as a commissioned officer then, if I may ask?"

Mr. Carnegie rested his head against the wall with a soft *thump*, as if the question troubled him. "I was orphaned last autumn, but I will not reach my majority for another two years. Worse, my father lost most of his fortune due to poor speculation, leaving me with little."

Leah's heart gave another wee lurch. So he *was* young . . . only nineteen.

"My uncle became my guardian after my father's death," he continued. "Unlike my pacifistic father, my uncle believes a man must do his duty and go to war when needed. I cannot say I relish the thought, but I must provide for myself and I have no interest in the Church. Therefore, the military is the only choice left. Uncle purchased me a commission in the 64th Foot, and here I am."

Living a life I never really wanted.

He didn't say the words, but she heard them nonetheless.

Leah knew that in-between feeling. When the smooth sailing of life crashed into a hard, unforgiving calamity.

"I ken a bit about change. My mother died two years past when my youngest brother was born—" She blink, blink, blinked before swallowing back her grief. "—and my father is still heartbroken over her loss. My younger brothers are too wee tae be without a mother, so I've had tae become their mamma."

Leah let out a slow breath, thinking about Malcolm and Ethan back home at Thistle Muir. How Malcolm, barely five, had *greited* and clung to her skirts as she walked to Uncle Leith's waiting carriage. How Ethan, scarcely two, had wailed his distress, reaching for her, fighting to get out of Cousin Elspeth's arms.

It had been too much. Leah had nearly turned back and stayed.

"Get on with ye. Go tae London," Elspeth had urged, holding Ethan tighter. As a lifelong spinster, her father's cousin had spent her years being passed like a parcel between relatives. "Get yourself a husband, lass."

Leah's father had stepped forward and pressed a soft kiss to her forehead.

"Aye," he said, voice gruff and eyes suspiciously bright. "Your mother wouldnae want ye tae be here. Go have a wee adventure. And if ye come back tae us married to some braw, young gentleman, so much the better."

Well, Fox Carnegie certainly fit the definition of a 'braw, young gentleman.'

"How challenging for you, to be raising your brothers," Mr. Carnegie replied, hair glinting in the firelight. "To take on so much, so young."

"You are kind tae say so, but we do what we must."

He sighed, a weary, body-worn sound. "You speak truth."

Silence descended.

A silence of kinship this time. A sense that, despite the differences in their upbringing and experiences, she and Fox Carnegie saw the world through a similar lens.

That they were, perhaps, cut from the same cloth.

He angled his head toward the door, listening intently. "We might finally be in the clear."

"Let me check."

Leah approached the door on light feet, pressing her ear against the dark oak.

Nothing.

Cautiously, she turned the lock and peered out into the hallway.

No one.

"How does it look?" he asked, his words close to her ear.

Leah jumped slightly, looking to him. Mr. Carnegie was scarcely a foot away. So close, she could see a faint mole to the right of his nose and count his individual eyelashes. So close, she could feel the heat of his body. So close, she would only have to lift onto tiptoe to press her mouth to his.

She blinked.

What had he asked?

"Good." Was her voice breathless? She *felt* breathless. "The coast is clear."

Nodding, he stooped down and hefted Lord Dennis upright once more. His lordship's eyes fluttered open and closed. Mr. Carnegie adjusted his hold, draping Dennis's elbow over his own shoulders and wrapping another arm around the man's waist.

"Thank you again for your kind company, Miss Penn-Leith," Mr. Carnegie whispered. "We shall remove ourselves, and let you see to your slumber."

He saluted her with his free hand and then he was gone, slipping out the door with his burden as soundlessly as he had entered it.

But the *feel* of Fox Carnegie lingered. A whiff of sandalwood. A sense of adventure in the air.

Sleep was decidedly long in coming.

Visit www.NicholeVan.com to get your copy of
Love Practically today and continue the story.

ABOUT THE AUTHOR

THE SHORT VERSION:

NICHOLE VAN IS a writer, photographer, designer and generally disorganized person. Though originally from the Rocky Mountains, she has lived all over the world, including Italy and the UK. She and her family recently returned to the US after spending six years in Scotland. Nichole currently lives in the heart of the Rockies with her husband and and three children.

THE LONG OVERACHIEVER VERSION:

AN INTERNATIONAL BESTSELLING author, Nichole Van is an artist who feels life is too short to only have one obsession. In former lives, she has been a contemporary dancer, pianist, art historian, choreographer, culinary artist and English professor.

Most notably, however, Nichole is an acclaimed photographer, winning over thirty international accolades for her work, including Portrait of the Year from WPPI in 2007. (Think Oscars for wedding and portrait photographers.) Her unique photography style has been featured in many magazines, including *Rangefinder* and *Professional Photographer*.

All that said, Nichole has always been a writer at heart. With an MA in English, she taught technical writing at Brigham Young University for ten years and has written more technical manuals than she can quickly count. She decided in late 2013 to start writing fiction and has since become an Amazon #1 bestselling author. Additionally, she has won a RONE award, as well as been a Whitney Award Finalist several years running. Her late 2018 release, *Seeing Miss Heartstone*, won the Whitney Award Winner for Best Historical Romance.

In 2017, Nichole, her husband and three children moved from the Rocky Mountains in the USA to Scotland. They lived there for six years—residing on the coast of eastern Scotland in an eighteenth century country house—before returning to the USA in 2023. Nichole currently lives in the heart of the Rockies, miles up a mountain canyon.

She is known as NicholeVan all over the web: Facebook, Instagram, Pinterest, etc. Visit http://www.NicholeVan.com to sign up for her author newsletter and be notified of new book releases.

If you enjoyed this book, please leave a short review on Amazon and/or Goodreads. Wonderful reviews are the elixir of life for authors. Even better than dark chocolate.

Made in the USA
Monee, IL
26 April 2025

16256754R00062